Tony Parsons, OAM, is a bestselling writer of rural Australian novels. He is the author of *The Call of the High Country*, *Return to the High Country*, *Valley of the White Gold* and *Silver in the Sun*. Tony has worked as a sheep and wool classer, journalist, news editor, rural commentator, consultant to major agricultural companies and an award-winning breeder of animals and poultry. He also established 'Karrawarra', one of the top kelpie studs in Australia, and was awarded the Order of Australia Medal for his contribution to the propagation of the Australian kelpie. Tony lives with his wife near Toowoomba and maintains a keen interest in kelpie breeding.

TONY PARSONS

Back to the Pilliga

ARENA
ALLEN&UNWIN

For my father

the late Ronald David Parsons, BEM

First published in 2013

Arena Books, an imprint of
Allen & Unwin
Sydney, Melbourne, Auckland, London

83 Alexander Street
Crows Nest NSW 2065
Australia
Phone: (61 2) 8425 0100
Fax: (61 2) 9906 2218
Email: info@allenandunwin.com
Web: www.allenandunwin.com

Cataloguing-in-Publication details are available
from the National Library of Australia
www.trove.nla.gov.au

ISBN 978 1 74331 052 6

Set in 11/18 pt Sabon by Post Pre-press Group, Australia
Printed and bound in Australia by Griffin Press

10 9 8 7 6 5 4 3 2 1

CHAPTER 1

There were four of us Sinclair children – three boys and a girl. Stuart was the oldest, my sister Flora came next, and I turned up just fifteen months after her. Our little brother, Kenneth, was the baby of the family.

Our father was a firm disciplinarian and never hesitated to give us a hiding if we failed to carry out our allotted tasks around the property, like feeding the horses, dogs and poultry. Flora and I copped our hidings in silence whereas at the first stroke of my father's belt or switch, Stuart would scream so loudly it usually brought my mother to his rescue.

Dad had an exalted view of his place in the Kamilaroi district, and anything that reflected on his reputation as an arbiter of good taste was anathema to him. This sometimes resulted in severe punishment for us if we stepped out of line. Being a girl didn't cut any ice with my father and he'd switch Flora with equal severity as us boys. Flora wasn't in any sense a 'bad' child but she was a real tomboy and my father thought that some of the things she did weren't 'ladylike'.

One of the worst hidings I received, and Flora copped it too, was when Stuart snitched on us for skinny-dipping in the creek. This was considered reprehensible behaviour but what made it even worse was that our school friend Fiona Cameron, a tomboy of the same ilk as my sister, was skinny dipping with us. This really inflamed the situation because my father thought it reflected badly on him and the way we had been raised. Quite apart from the hidings for skinny-dipping, Flora and I were given additional tasks to do and received no pocket money for three months.

What made the punishment even more onerous was that we were given some of Stuart's jobs in addition to our own while he kept on receiving his usual pocket money.

Although I was only a boy at the time that Stuart snitched on us, afterwards I harboured a residual dislike for him and I didn't like working with him on any kind of task. This wasn't because he was lazy or lacked interest in the activities associated with a big grazing property but because of his personality. He was continually trying to ingratiate himself with our father and it didn't concern him how badly we appeared. He'd sometimes lie to Father that he'd had to do one of my jobs. In fact I rarely ever skipped a job and covered for Stuart on several occasions.

The first time I gave Stuart a bleeding nose was when he fibbed about riding his pony. Father had found it lame and told me to tell Stuart he wasn't to ride it until the vet had looked at it. Stuart rode the pony and later told Father that I hadn't given him the message.

'You're a liar as well as being a snitch,' I told him before punching him in the face. 'Don't ever ask me to do anything for you again.'

I was punished for giving him the bleeding nose but it was worth it for the satisfaction it gave me. From that day on neither Flora nor me told Stuart any of our 'secrets' – like the time we set duck eggs under one of Father's prize Australorp hens. He never did discover how that happened.

Stuart modelled himself on our father who, despite being respected for his ownership of Kamilaroi, was not well liked in the district.

As well as being one of the reasons for my dislike of Stuart, the day we went skinny-dipping was also the day I realised that girls were made differently to boys.

CHAPTER 2

When I was growing up on Kamilaroi it was the second largest property in the general Coonabarabran area and was as much a part of the district as the adjacent Pilliga Scrub.

The first rule on Kamilaroi was that my father's word was law and couldn't be disputed under any circumstances. As well as dominating his family, my father tried to dominate every organisation with which he became involved, including the old Pastures Protection Board and the local show society. Though not much loved, my father held a privileged position in the district because of his ownership of Kamilaroi. There were people who sucked up to Father to get his business, which sometimes worked and sometimes didn't. But if a business got on the wrong side of him, that was the end of the relationship.

Father was a very much larger than life character. It wasn't that he had a great sense of humour because he had very little of that commodity. The fact was that he had a great presence. He looked like an aristocrat and he behaved like one. He was about six feet in height with wide shoulders and a trim waist which didn't thicken substantially until he was an old man. He had a face you could never forget because of his brow and his keen grey eyes. He had the brow of an intellectual though he didn't possess a brilliant mind. I'd say he was smart and he ran Kamilaroi like a well oiled machine. He cultivated a moustache which certainly suited him. He was a martinet and he would have been a tough man to serve under in the 2nd AIF.

He'd had to take over the management of Kamilaroi as a quite young man when his father died as the result of war injuries in France. I reckon my father could have outwalked any man I ever knew. He walked with a springy kind of stride that ate up the ground. He had a fearsome reputation and when he came into the shed at shearing time all levity ceased. Father would have a look at the wool in the bins and then he'd go outside and cast his eyes over the shorn sheep in each shearer's pen. If there were sheep cut about or unevenly shorn he'd have a word with the shearing contractor and that shearer would be replaced. I only ever knew of one contractor who argued the point with Father and he lost the shed.

As a boy growing up on a large sheep, cattle and grain property, I belonged to what was probably the last generation of children whose grazier fathers had real 'clout'. The wool boom of the fifties was only a memory and the influence of the bush expressed via the old Country Party (now the National Party) had been very considerably reduced. The old bush socio-economic way of life was still there but the edifice was crumbling. Low wool prices, the 1975 slump in prices for beef cattle, indifferent seasons and higher costs were having a catastrophic effect on the financial viability of farming. Some of the great pastoral companies saw the writing on the wall and sold their historic properties. But many well managed properties continued to do all right, including Kamilaroi. There was still a good demand for our stud sheep and bulls, and my father also raced a couple of thoroughbred horses.

I've got to say that if it hadn't been for my mother and Flora my childhood would have been hard to take. Mum was a very sweet person with a great deal of love to give, which she showered unreservedly on us children. She was always there to greet us when we arrived home from school, and the period between getting home and having dinner was a very special one because Father was either out on the run or away at one of his many meetings so we had Mum to ourselves. After we'd finished our chores we'd sit around the kitchen table and eat Mum's incomparable shortbread, gingerbread men and sometimes hot pancakes. Mum would always ask how school had been and whether we had any problems with things like maths because she always had.

Mum came from a wealthy grazing family and why she chose our father as her husband was always a mystery to me because I doubt very much that she ever loved him. I have great difficulty accepting that she would have been party to an arranged marriage even though girls of her class had been expected to make good marriages. After they married, women like my mother were supposed to run their big homes and have children. They certainly weren't meant to be engaged in anything as plebeian as working in an outside job. Funny that because in only a few years the definition of a viable farmer would become a farmer who had a wife with a job!

It seemed to me that my mother was a very special kind of woman; she was different. It wasn't until after I left Kamilaroi and inhabited the wider world beyond its boundaries that I realised what made Mum different. It was style. Mum endowed everything she did with style. It wasn't laid on with a trowel but part of her overall captivating personality. She was lovely; a brunette with natural waves and hazel eyes. And she was tall, only a couple of inches shorter than my father. Her movements, whether seen in the kitchen or outside in the garden, were always graceful.

Tradesmen loved her and would do almost anything for her because she treated them as if they were knights of the realm. There was always a cup of tea and a scone or a piece of cake for every tradesman who came to Kamilaroi. It infuriated my father but his sternest words had no effect on my mother who carried on as if she hadn't heard him. I never heard a bad word said about her and her charm and natural warmth did a lot to offset my father's stand-offish image. My father might have been a pastoral patrician but my mother was a princess.

I wasn't very old when I recognised that my father didn't have much time for women generally. He behaved as if they'd been created to become wives and mothers and not to intrude beyond those areas. He told me once that women had innate problems and couldn't be considered on the same plane as men. He never departed from this view; in fact he became even more intractable about it as he got older. This was very strange given that he'd married such a smart, capable and caring woman as my mother.

Though not as dismissive of women as Father, my brother Stuart had a high-handed manner with women which often rubbed them up the wrong way. Although he'd tried to model himself on Father, he was but a pale imitation of him, not possessing his aura or physical presence. Stuart was just below medium height and although not bad looking, he was not a man you'd look at twice unless he was on a horse. He had a lovely seat on a horse and it was something to see him and my father riding together. I wasn't in their class as a horseman though I loved horses.

Stuart's big problem was that he spoke down to everyone. Because he was up himself, he became the butt of jokes. I tried to ignore him as much as possible though this wasn't always possible because we often had to work together in the sheep and cattle yards. Stuart wasn't a great one for the girls because he spent most of his time trying to please Father.

I took the opposite direction – there was never a time when I didn't like girls. From the first, I was very close to Flora, who was a ripper of a sister and was to remain my best friend all my life. Luke Stirling was my best mate but Flora was my best friend and there is a difference. Flora wouldn't hesitate to chip me if she thought I needed it but I knew she did it for my own good.

Because of the location of Kamilaroi (it was named for the great Aboriginal tribe that once occupied a large area of northern New South Wales) we kids grew up with a fair knowledge of the unique character of the area around us, which included the vast Pilliga Scrub. You couldn't drive in any direction from our property without traversing the scrub or land that had been cleared of scrub. The Pilliga had been the source of limitless tonnes of cypress pine and ironbark for both timber millers and landowners like my father. Virtually every stick of timber used on Kamilaroi was sourced from it.

For a kid like me, the Pilliga Scrub was much more than a never-failing source of timber, however: it was a place of mystery and challenge. Some of my very earliest memories are of listening to stories of strange happenings in the Pilliga Scrub. It was said that black panthers roamed there and numerous bodies were buried there. But by far the most stories were about stolen livestock being taken to the scrub, some for re-sale or simply to be butchered. So the Pilliga Scrub held a kind of awed fascination for me.

Soon after I gained my driver's licence I began to explore the roads and timber tracks in the Pilliga Scrub, often following the route taken by Jimmy and Joe Governor during their violent rampage – which included nine murders and the rape of a fifteen-year-old girl. Sometimes referred to as the Breelong Blacks, the Governors were actually half caste and used rifles, shotguns, tomahawks and nulla nullas in their crimes. They were eventually tracked by bloodhounds and expert black trackers from Fraser Island before Joe was shot and killed north of Singleton by a man called John Wilkinson. Jimmy was shot in the Wingham area and then taken by steamer to Sydney where he was hanged at Darlinghurst gaol.

Once, as I was driving up a bush track in the Pilliga, a man stepped out of the scrub holding a rifle, which he pointed at me before telling me to scram. Heart thumping, I backed the ute up as fast as I could until I found a place where I could turn around and then hightailed it out of there. When I told Father about the man with the rifle he said he'd report it to the police though they would have Buckley's chance of locating a lone man in a million acres of scrub.

Even without all the stories, the Pilliga Scrub could be a spooky place to be in at night. It was probably the thickness of the pines and their blackness when the sun went down that made it appear so eerie. With nightfall in the scrub came the orchestra of the pines and the sounds of crickets singing in the mulch, along with the coughing of koalas and the monotonous crying of mopokes. For anyone not raised in the bush or lacking exposure to noises of the night, the Pilliga could be a frightening experience. Later, years later, I discovered that scientists had proven that Aboriginal occupancy of the area could be traced back 21,000 years.

It was always understood that my father expected Stuart, Kenneth and I to return to Kamilaroi after we finished school. My father intended to expand our landholdings by buying at least one neighbouring property, his view being that you could never own too much land and that in Australia most holdings were too small to be really viable.

Kenneth turned out to be very bright and his school results were so good that my mother suggested he go on to university and study veterinary science, since he'd always been good with animals. Initially there was a great argument between my parents about the merits of Kenneth going to university, mainly because Mum had suggested it. Later, Father acknowledged that there'd be definite advantages to having a vet in the family. As well as helping generally with our livestock, Kenneth might be able to help set up and run the artificial breeding programs my father wanted to introduce. Despite his many personal faults, my father was a superb manager and he kept on top of all the latest developments in farming.

Unlike Stuart, I had mixed feelings about returning to Kamilaroi after boarding school. I liked the land well enough but the thought of working cheek by jowl with my father and Stuart didn't appeal greatly. After the comparative 'freedom' of boarding school, it would be hard to endure my father's bullying ways and the constant tension in the air that resulted from him being such a tyrant. Also, as I'd grown older, whenever I came home on holidays I hated the way he spoke to Mum on the rare occasions she opposed him. He never accepted that she knew anything about the property or what might be best for us.

So I felt very ambivalent when I did end up returning to Kamilaroi after school. I loved many aspects of the life, and there were things about living on a big property that couldn't be replicated elsewhere, like the way the property came to life at shearing time and at harvesting. It was great to look at the big bins of wool in the shearing shed to assess whether the clip was better or worse than in previous years. I always found mustering a joy too, especially with a good casting paddock dog. Working with a new horse was also exciting. We bred our own horses at Kamilaroi and they were handled by a local horse breaker. There was usually a bit of ginger in the young horses even after they'd been broken in so they took handling for a while. I particularly enjoyed the days when the ram buyers came to inspect the rams and they'd discuss spinning quality, colour and cut. The bull buyers spent more money on individual animals but there was less passion in their selections.

At weekends I played cricket for the district side, which I loved doing. I had been well coached at boarding school and I'd been the opening batsman in a strong team which had attracted the attention of local cricket clubs. I was disappointed to have to turn down invitations to play for a couple of Sydney grade sides when I left school.

A particularly enjoyable aspect of returning to Kamilaroi after spending six years at an all-male boarding school was spending more time with women. I especially enjoyed seeing the Cameron sisters, Sheila and Fiona (Flora's childhood skinny-dipping mate), whom I'd known for most of my life. Though both lived in Sydney, they came home regularly during term breaks and holidays.

Fiona, who had always excelled at school, was studying medicine at Sydney University. Sheila, two years younger than Fiona, was nursing at Royal Prince Alfred Hospital in Camperdown. Whenever they came home I saw a lot of both of them because Sheila, in particular, was very close to Flora and we often got together at the pub for a drink. Both sisters were attractive looking women with appealing personalities. Fiona had a very lively intelligence, a strong personality and was very forthright in her opinions. Though also clever, Sheila had no desire to push her point of view on to others and though very warm and inquiring was a little over-shadowed by Fiona's charisma.

For a year or more I enjoyed spending time with both Fiona and Sheila whenever they were back in the district. Then, one night when I drove Fiona home it just so happened that her parents were away in Sydney and we had the place to ourselves. Fiona took me by the hand, led me into her bedroom and began taking off her clothes. The last time I'd seen her without clothes was the day Stuart had snitched on us for skinny dipping in the creek and naturally she looked radically different now.

After we'd kissed for a while I told Fiona I didn't have a condom.

'That's all right. I've had a diaphragm fitted,' she told me.

Sex with Fiona was a complete revelation, despite my inexperience. Fiona and I went on to have sex twice more that evening and by the end of the night I was totally smitten with her.

The Pilliga Scrub was to come in very handy around this time because it wasn't easy to get away from Kamilaroi or to find suitable places for our trysts. There was such a vast area of it and it was so thickly covered with timber that you could go to places where there was no danger of prying eyes while you made love. Despite Fiona's expensive upbringing she had no hesitation in disrobing and having sex among the pines. She knew far more about sex than me and was always encouraging me to try some new technique. Looking back on it now it's amazing that I never wondered at the apparent depth of Fiona's sexual experience.

Flora, who was never afraid to call a spade a shovel, asked me how I was getting on with Fiona. I told her I was getting on very well and that it was highly likely that we'd get engaged some time during the year.

'I'd have a good long think about that, Lachie. If you want my opinion you'd be wiser to concentrate on Sheila than Fiona,' said Flora.

I looked at her in amazement. 'Why do you say that?' I asked.

'Because you and I have known each other since we were kids, and I've grown up with Fiona. She's very ambitious and wants to become a medical specialist. She's unlikely to want to come back here to be a grazier's wife and I can't see her fitting in with what you want. I don't want either of you to be unhappy, Lachie, and I think you will be if you marry each other,' said Flora.

When I remained silent, though clearly uncomfortable, Flora continued.

'Fiona has always got everything she wanted. She starred at whatever sports she chose and excelled academically. She went out with the captain of the First Eleven when she was at school and her first boyfriend at university was one of her lecturers, an associate professor. You're the shining star of the district, Lachie. You're the top local cricketer, you're from a wealthy family, you're bright and handsome and well liked. I know of at least ten women who think you're terrific and would love to marry you. Fiona definitely cares for and is attracted to you, but the fact that you're so sought after is at least part of your attraction for her. It's Fiona all over,' she said.

'Why do you say that?' I asked.

'I know Fiona so well,' she said. 'I'm sure you're thoroughly enjoying yourselves but what's going to happen when Fiona goes back to university? She'll expect to see you fairly regularly. And you know what Father is like and he won't like you skipping off to spend time in Sydney.'

'I'm not sure I want to be tied to Kamilaroi forever,' I said, annoyed. 'Father can't just assume I'll devote my entire life to it. Sons have girlfriends who they want to see. I'll sort that out,' I said.

'Having a fling with Fiona is one thing but marrying her is quite another. She has no intention of having children early in her career if at all. Have you discussed this with her?' she asked.

'It's a bit early to be talking about kids,' I said, though I'd always envisaged having some.

'Lachie, I know Fiona. You only *think* you know her. You're certainly not taking the long view – or even the short view for that matter. Where do you plan to live if you marry Fiona? There's no way she'll want to come back to Coonabarabran permanently to be a country GP,' said Flora.

'You know that for a fact, do you?' I asked.

'I know that when Fi finishes medicine she wants to do a post-graduate degree so she can specialise. She might come back here occasionally to see her Mum and Dad but she definitely won't be living here. Have you discussed this stuff at all?' Flora asked.

'Not so we could nail anything down,' I admitted. 'The fact of the matter is that I'm not sure I want to stay here either. I like working on the land well enough but Father and Stuart are hard to stomach and the tension at home is really getting to me at the moment. You know what it's like.'

'What would you do if you left Kamilaroi?' Flora asked.

'I've thought about joining the police force. One of my friends from school became a cop and he reckons if you're good at sport they give you plenty of time off to play. I'm not saying I'd want to become a cop forever but it might be all right for a few years,' I said.

'The police force? What does Fiona think about that?' Flora asked.

'Fiona thinks I should go to university but there's nothing there that really appeals to me. And I wouldn't want to be in a boring nine to five job. If I decided to go into the police force I'm sure she'd accept the idea,' I said.

Flora looked at me dubiously. 'I wouldn't count on it, Lachie. If you join the police force you could get posted to Woop Woop for some time and you'd be separated from Fiona. That isn't a great recipe for a successful marriage. You've always got on so well with Sheila and ultimately you're much better suited to each other. Also, she wants to come back here and, with nurses being so much in demand, she could probably get a position at Coona hospital so you'd have extra income. But I assure you that Fiona won't be coming back here for any length of time.'

I was having too good a time with Fiona to take Flora seriously. Fiona and I went everywhere together and we were having a lot of fun. There were parties, barbecues, swimming excursions, polocrosse tournaments and picnic races and then there was Fiona and all that she offered. I had never enjoyed life so much.

We both realised that the university holidays were quickly coming to an end and Fiona would have to head back soon but we pushed that into the background and when it happened, it happened.

I felt very down in the dumps when Fiona drove away. I'd have felt much worse if I hadn't been kept so busy on the property. Quite apart from all the usual jobs, I'd taken on just about all of the tractor work. I was my own boss in the cabin of the tractor and able to keep right away from my father and Stuart. Although most of Kamilaroi country was on the light side and didn't produce big yields of wheat, it was very good oats country and we grew a lot of oats. Some we utilised for grazing, especially for ewes with lambs, and cows with calves, and some we stored in our silos. The tractor work took up a lot of time and we had all the work associated with having over 30,000 sheep, 1000 head of breeding cows, bred our own stock horses and Father raced a couple of thoroughbreds.

There weren't many spare moments to think because there were always ram and bull buyers to look after. In the days when labour was less expensive we'd done all the lamb-marking and mulesing ourselves but now we brought in a team of casuals to do these tasks. This lightened the load considerably but we still had plenty to do. It was a source of great satisfaction to Father that he could work Kamilaroi for most of the time with members of his own family – and Kenneth was a great help when he was home from school.

I loved Kamilaroi and I would have loved it even more if I hadn't had to put up with Father and Stuart. I suppose that was what made Fiona even more attractive, the contrast between some- one so agreeable and two men who weren't. In fact all the women I knew rated very highly in my life. Quite apart from Fiona there was Mum and then there was Flora and Sheila. These women, like so many of their sex, managed the really important building blocks of life, uppermost of which was family. If it hadn't been for my brother Kenneth I would have been thoroughly disappointed with the men of my family.

CHAPTER 3

I stuck it out at Kamilaroi for four years after school, during which Stuart, to my amazement, met and married a lovely woman called Nicole, who was half-French and had a kind of sultry beauty. Nicole was modelling at a fashion show when Stuart met her and it wasn't long before they decided to get married. Looking back, I wonder if Nicole weighed up her future as a model in the very competitive world of fashion against the security marrying Stuart offered. Also, despite lacking a bit of height, Stuart was quite dashing back then.

Unfortunately marriage – even to such an attractive and likeable woman as Nicole – didn't improve Stuart. Like my father, he continued to get people offside by talking down to them.

I was very proud of my younger brother, Kenneth, and we got on like a house on fire. As well as being naturally academic, he'd worked hard at school, and was an extremely promising cricketer. Whenever he came home during the summer break we spent countless hours practising cricket together. An all rounder, he was an excellent pace bowler and a handy batsman.

By the time Kenneth finished school, Flora had already met and married a great bloke called Laurie Stratton and they'd bought a house in town. Stuart and Nicole had also married and had their own place about half a mile from the old Kamilaroi homestead. As Mum had hoped, Kenneth had got the marks to enrol in vet science but came home for the summer holidays before uni started. Because he was such a good bowler our cricket coach got him to come along to practice sessions and bowl to us in the nets. Within days of him coming along for the first time the blokes in the team had dubbed him 'the kid' and he was considered one of us. Naturally, he was crazy keen to come and watch us when we made it into the final of the area cricket competition.

Unhappy at the amount of time Kenneth and I were spending playing and practising cricket, on the night before the final Father insisted that Kenneth get the sheep in the shed for crutching before he was allowed to head into town to watch the cricket.

Father set off early on the morning of the final, having made an appointment to look at some rams at a stud near Coolah, and Kenneth decided he'd come and watch the final before heading home to round up the sheep. By mid-afternoon I was on 73 not out and we needed another 100 runs to win. Kenneth stayed and stayed, unable to drag himself away, given the excitement and suspense. When Father arrived home to find that Kenneth wasn't there and the sheep hadn't been brought into the yards, he was furious. He rang the club, and got someone to summons Kenneth to the phone before tearing strips off him, shouting at him to get himself home and do the job he'd been instructed to do.

I was still batting when Kenneth tore off home on one of the

Kamilaroi bikes. After winning the final for the first time in several years we were all celebrating with a beer when my captain was called to the phone. When he came back he took me aside and told me that Kenneth had been killed in an accident. The police later told me that Kenneth must have been going flat strap to have been thrown the distance he was when his bike hit a 'roo. They assured me he would have died instantly.

The reality of Kenneth's death hit everyone in our family hard, but particularly me and Mum. Kenneth had been Mum's youngest and they'd shared a particular love of and empathy for animals. He'd always been able to make her laugh and she'd always maintained a soft spot for him. For me, Kenneth had been my mate and we'd shared a love of playing, watching and talking about sport, and we'd always hoped to play cricket together one day. I was absolutely devastated that he'd died needlessly as a result of our father's inflexibility.

When I got home the day Kenneth died everyone was there – my father and mother, Stuart and Nicole, and Flora – who had rushed out to Kamilaroi when Nicole phoned her with the terrible news.

Mum and Flora and I hugged and cried together for a long time, unable to believe we'd never see Kenneth grow up and fulfil his potential. And though I knew my father hadn't meant to cause Kenneth's death and must have been feeling guilty and grief-stricken, I was so angry and anguished I just lost it with him, hitting him with the full force of my fury, telling him I'd never forgive him for Kenneth's death. I raged at him about his inflexibility and how his need to play the big strict Father had contributed to Kenneth's death. Every time he attempted to say something I told him to shut his face.

'You can't talk to Father like that,' Stuart said at some stage.

'You shut your face too,' I snarled, before proceeding to tell him precisely what I thought of him. 'I've hung on here for Mum's sake but the thought of staying here and working any longer with you and Father after this is more than I can stomach. This is the stone cold finish. You can have your precious Kamilaroi. I'm leaving.'

'Lachie, you should wait until you've cooled down before you make such a huge decision,' said Flora.

'Yes and I don't see how you can blame Father for Kenneth's death. He was asked to do a job and he wasn't here to do it,' said Stuart.

'You miserable apology for a man. You've crawled to Father ever since you first opened your eyes and you're still crawling to him. You both knew how keen Kenneth was to watch the final and neither of you offered to bring in the sheep for him. Some father, some brother. You're welcome to each other. I'm packing a bag and then I'm leaving. I'm so sorry, Mum, I wish I could stay longer because of you but I just can't do it anymore after all this.'

With that, I stormed out of the room, walked to my bedroom and started to throw some clothes into one of my old school bags. Mum came into the room soon after and, without saying anything, helped me pack.

When we'd finished, Mum and I hugged and cried some more. I apologised to her that I was leaving, saying, 'You're a bottler, Mum, but I've got to go.'

'I understand, Lachie . . .' Mum said, with tears running down her cheeks.

'I'll be there for you at the funeral, Mum,' I said, kissing and hugging her before leaving.

When I got outside, Flora was standing beside my ute.

'You'd better come and stay with Laurie and me until the funeral is sorted out. You're not fit company to be with anyone else right now,' she said.

That was Flora. She was a true blue woman and she could handle me better than any other woman I'd ever met. Laurie was an accountant who hadn't known much about the land when they met but was awfully good at figures. Flora soon schooled him in the ways of the land. They hadn't been married long and still had stars in their eyes for each other. I'd always expected Flora to marry a bloke on the land but I didn't have any qualms about Laurie. He was a very decent and likeable bloke and I'd got on very well with him right from the start.

'Thanks, Flora,' I said. 'Let's go before I do something I'll be sorry for later.'

CHAPTER 4

Kenneth's funeral was a grim affair with a huge number of mourners in attendance to pay their respects. Kenneth had been one of the most popular young fellows in the district and his death, and the manner of it, was seen as a terrible tragedy. Given the entire cricket team knew about the lead-up to his death, it wasn't long before most of the district were aware Kenneth had been killed while hurrying home to obey my Father's angry instructions. Because of this the sympathy extended towards my father was muted compared to the outpouring of support for my mother who was so well liked.

Father arrived at the funeral looking so ashen-faced and bereft that it was hard not to feel sorry for him. Mum was distraught throughout the funeral and Flora and I needed to support her to keep standing at times. Stuart looked stunned and Nicole cried a lot because she'd been very fond of Kenneth. Fiona, who had rushed up for the funeral, held my arm throughout the service and her presence and support was a great comfort to me. In fact, if it hadn't been for her and Flora I don't think I'd have got through the funeral. It was very tough for me to get through the eulogy because every word struck at my heart but when I sat down she squeezed my hand, kissed me and said Kenneth would have loved what I'd said about him. Looking back, Kenneth's death was the lowest point of my life.

After the wake as Fiona and I prepared to leave town, I talked with Mum about why I felt I had to leave. She knew how strained my relationship with Father and Stuart was and how hard it would be for us to work together on Kamilaroi but couldn't understand why I had to leave the district altogether.

'Being here would be a constant reminder of Kenneth's death – it'd never feel the same hanging out with friends or playing cricket here. And Fiona's future lies in Sydney. It's best for all concerned that I go, Mum. I hate leaving you, especially now, and I wouldn't be able to do it if you didn't have Flora close by,' I said.

Fiona remained wonderfully supportive in the aftermath of Kenneth's death. She took time off university to be with me and she invited me to come down and live with her in Sydney. We discussed what I would do if I moved down there and, whatever her private feelings about it, she was supportive of my desire to join the police force, perhaps knowing it would provide me with some distraction from my grief about Kenneth.

I felt a huge sense of relief as we left Coonabarabran and while I drove I turned my thoughts to the future. I didn't see being in the police force as a long-term proposition because I knew, even then, I'd eventually want to get back on the land. I couldn't see how I was going to do it and nor could I see how it would fit in with

Fiona's plans. She hadn't talked a lot about what she hoped to do other than to say she wanted to specialise.

Shortly after I arrived in Sydney I went ahead and joined the police force. And though originally one of the things that had appealed to me about becoming a policeman was the inducements they offered for sporting types, I was never again able to work up much enthusiasm for playing sport after Kenneth died. Instead, I threw myself into my new role as a police officer. I soon realised that Fiona's future as a specialist lay in Sydney where the big hospitals offered the latest in medical procedures. And though I did do a stint away in the Central West it wasn't long before I transferred to plain clothes work back in Sydney and became a detective sergeant.

Having grown up using firearms I was not a bad shot, though up until I joined the police all my shooting had been with a rifle. I'd even done a bit of competitive rifle shooting. After becoming a detective I practised very hard with hand guns, which assumed greater importance than rifles in a detective's life. Still, funnily enough, after years of identifying individual sheep and cattle and learning to read the bush I had a keen eye for detail with regard to people.

Fiona and I decided to get married when she completed her medical degree and, with me still unable to face the thought of going back to Coonabarabran for any reason, we had our wedding ceremony in Sydney.

Father and Stuart didn't come down for the wedding. Nicole and her girls were there though I learnt later that there'd been an unholy row between Nicole and Stuart about them coming. Mum and Flora were the two that mattered and they were there.

There was quite a contingent of other people from Coonabarabran because the Camerons had been prominent landowners there for generations. Sheila was one of Fiona's bridesmaids and I asked Luke Stirling – who had become one of my good mates in the force – to be my best man, though I'd always envisaged Kenneth in that role.

Fiona had graduated from medicine with first class honours and her parents had bought her a house on the North Shore which we moved into straight after our honeymoon. Within weeks of our wedding Fiona started out as an intern and her life soon became completely dominated by work. The hours she and the other interns were required to work amazed me and it seemed like a wonder they could stand up, let alone treat gravely injured people, by the time their shifts were coming to a close. Our sex life – which had always been a focal point of our relationship – waned under the weight of Fiona's constant exhaustion.

After her period as an intern Fiona started postgraduate work so that she could specialise in heart surgery. It was during this time that she seemed to change from the girl I'd known back in Coonabarabran. She'd never put much effort into cooking – which had never greatly bothered me – but rather than the two of us going out together, her idea of a good night out was for us to go to a restaurant with some of her medical colleagues. Their conversation was often way above my head so I usually felt like a fish out of water.

Whenever I raised the idea of having children, Fiona said there'd be plenty of time to have kids once she was established as a heart surgeon. I was very keen on having kids and I dreamt of us having a son called Kenneth who I could teach how to play cricket and rugby. Whenever I thought about bringing up kids I wanted to give them everything I'd been denied growing up. Though growing up in the country had been great I was glad we'd be living in the city only insofar as our kids wouldn't have to be sent away to school.

I think I continued to wilfully ignore Flora's warning that Fiona wouldn't necessarily want to have any children. After establishing herself in heart surgery Fiona began to hint that I leave the police force. Though she never really said it, it was clear to me that she thought there were a lot more desirable things I could be doing.

'You could buy into a business,' she kept telling me.

'What kind of business do you have in mind?' I asked her on one occasion.

'The father of one of my colleagues owns a company that supplies purified water to businesses. It's quite lucrative and he's got cancer and wants to sell it,' said Fiona.

I groaned. 'What makes you think I'd prefer selling water to the police work I do which is at least interesting.'

'You wouldn't have to do the actual work, only look after the administration. Your employees would do the actual work,' she said.

'No,' I said emphatically.

I thought I was doing quite well in the police force and I had a great partner in the bloke who'd been my best man, Luke Stirling. I had no desire to change my job for something I knew nothing about while Fiona went happily on doing what she wanted.

Married life with Fiona wasn't at all like I'd expected it to be. The crisis point in our marriage came when I was shot while Luke and I were apprehending Ben 'Bud' Hollis. Hollis was a bad egg, who was in the top ten of Australia's most wanted criminals. After two stints in the clink he had sworn never to be taken again.

Following a tip-off, Luke and I had located Hollis and we were watching a house in Chatswood while waiting for back-up. Hollis had a partner and he sent her out of the house and we thought she might have gone for food. A few minutes later a car came screaming up the street and Hollis burst out of the house with a pistol in one hand and a sawn-off shotgun in the other. Luke gunned our Holden into life and drove it up the street to block the other car's getaway. Hollis fired two shots, both of which hit the Holden and as I got out to fire from behind our vehicle I was hit in the shoulder. As Hollis brought up the shotgun to fire at Luke I steadied my arm against the Holden and squeezed off a single shot. Hollis dropped.

'Get the woman, Luke. I'll watch Hollis,' I shouted. Watching was about all I could do because of the terrible pain in my shoulder. But Hollis didn't require any watching because he was dead and Luke soon had his handcuffs on the woman. He called an ambulance for me by which time our back-up had arrived.

Both the police and the media praised Luke and me for dealing with Hollis. He'd had the firepower to deal with both of us which had certainly been his intention.

Fiona was great while I was in hospital and looked after me well when I first came home. However I had only been recuperating for a couple of weeks before she started pressuring me to leave the force again.

'You aren't thinking of staying in the force now, are you? You're going to have a stiff shoulder indefinitely and they'll probably put you in some dreary office job you'll hate,' said Fiona.

'I'll be as right as rain after a couple of months of gym work and physio,' I said.

'It's too dangerous. You're putting yourself at risk all the time,' she said.

'Someone has to do it and I think I'm good at my job,' I said.

'Being good at it didn't prevent you from being shot. You're going up against the very worst type of criminal and some of them have no compunction about shooting policemen. I've had enough of it, Lachie. Resign and do something else,' she said.

'If I resign it will be to work for myself in the same field,' I said.

'You mean as a private detective?' she asked.

'That's right,' I said.

'That's worse than what you're doing now. Getting evidence for divorces. Ugh,' she said.

'What it really boils down to is that me being a cop, private or otherwise, is bad for your image. That's the real reason you want me out of the force, isn't it? I'm an embarrassment to you,' I said harshly.

I could see that I'd hit the target and that Fiona didn't appreciate being put on the spot.

'The fact of the matter is that we're not compatible, Lachie. We never have been except in bed and the magic's been missing from that for some time. I'm largely to blame. If you'd married Sheila, you'd have had a family and been much happier,' she said.

'Maybe I should have married Sheila. I don't reckon she'd go running around with other blokes behind my back,' I said, finally raising a long-held suspicion of mine.

Fiona's face flamed and I knew I'd scored a hit.

'When your shoulder is right I want you to leave, Lachie. Can you get the tenants out of the Neutral Bay house?' she asked.

Not long after Kenneth's death my mother had bequeathed a considerable amount of money to Flora, Stuart and me. She was a wealthy woman in her own right because as well as having been left a pile of money – most of which had been invested for her – she also received an ongoing share of the income from her family's properties. I think in the aftermath of Kenneth's death she'd wanted to do something for all us kids to make life a bit easier financially.

The money Mum sent me was enough to make a large down payment on a big old house in Neutral Bay. The house and grounds had been let go and both needed quite a lot of attention. I paid a charitable organisation to clean up the grounds then I moved in and gradually cleaned up the inside of the house and did some essential repair work. When Fiona and I had married she was keen to remain in the house her parents had bought her on the North Shore because it was easier to get to the hospital she was working at. So, whenever a tenant moved out of Neutral Bay I'd do some work on it, one room at a time. First a bedroom and then the kitchen. Fiona never contributed a hand's turn to the restoration as she was studying most of the time.

'I'll find out,' I said.

'Good. Whatever the case I want you to move out as soon as you're feeling up to it. You're still in good shape and young enough to enjoy children if you happen to find a woman you like. Twelve months' separation is sufficient for divorce. I don't want anything from you, Lachie. I want our separation to be amicable so I hope you won't bring my friendship with Richard into the divorce proceedings,' she said.

'No, I won't do that,' I said firmly. 'I'm sorry it's had to end like this, Fiona. I realise now that our marriage has been going downhill for a while but I suppose I'd been hoping things would improve.'

I hated the idea of divorce, because any way you looked at it it meant failure, but I'd learned to look at things as they were and not as I'd like them to be, and clearly Fiona and I wanted different things in life.

After I'd been patched up I went back to work and stayed with the police force until after the divorce came through before resigning. Some of the chiefs tried very hard to persuade me to reconsider my decision. My immediate boss, Detective Superintendent Ballinger, tried hardest of all.

'You've got a great future here, Lachie,' he said. 'You could go right to the top.'

I had a lot of time for Ballinger. He was a top bloke and a great cop. He had lost his wife to cancer and raised their daughter, Alison, by himself. Alison was a very clever woman who, coincidentally, had gone through medical school with Fiona.

'It's time to move on, Super,' I said. 'Fiona blames the Force for our separation and to a certain extent she's right.'

'I hate to lose you, Lachie,' said Ballinger. 'I mean that. If you're determined to leave I can't stop you and I hope it turns out for the best. Let me know if there's any way I can help you.'

'Thanks, Super. I appreciate your offer. Maybe I'll be able to help you occasionally,' I said.

'How's that?' he asked.

'I'm setting up as a security adviser. I'll be doing other work but I'll be fairly choosey with what I take on. If I ever hear anything to your advantage I'll pass it on via Luke,' I said.

'I see,' he said and drummed his fingers on his desk. 'Keep in touch, Lachie,' he said.

'I will, Super. I'll get Luke to bring you a fish or two,' I said with a grin. We shook hands and I was almost to the door when he called me back.

'Alison was asking after you, Lachie. She told me to say hello.'

I looked at him and nodded. 'How's she doing?'

'She's specialising in paediatrics. You should give her a call when you get settled down,' Ballinger said with a slight smile.

'I might get to like her too much, Super. No more career women for me. Once bitten, forever shy,' I said.

So I walked out of police headquarters as my own man. I couldn't truthfully say that I was disenchanted with the force, though I was frustrated by the fact that many criminals were being treated too leniently. I was also aware that some prominent officers were on the take but this wasn't a situation unique to the New South Wales force. But by and large the majority of the State's police officers did a great job and often under very trying circumstances.

I left the police force with a lot of experience of crims, a scar on my right shoulder and a medal. Before I settled into my new role as security adviser and private investigator, I decided to travel around Australia, which was something I'd always wanted to do, though I hadn't anticipated doing it solo. During my trip, which I now look back on as a highlight of my life, I began to take a real interest in photography as distinct from simply taking pictures. I made a lot of lonely camps and had plenty of time to think about what I was doing with the rest of my life and what I hoped to achieve.

I decided that before too long I'd sell the Neutral Bay place and go back to the bush. I wanted to buy a property, get married and work up the property with my wife – if that's what she wanted to do. It wouldn't matter if there was no great fortune to be made or even if we had to battle a bit. And we'd have kids and we'd rear them with love and consideration. That was what I'd had from my mother and I wanted to be a very different type of father than my own.

CHAPTER 5

Kenneth's death and my departure from Kamilaroi affected my parents a great deal, though in different ways. It was a real heart-wrenching time for my mother who was grief-stricken about Kenneth being cut down in his prime with such a promising future ahead of him. She also missed having me close by as we'd always got on well and been each other's allies. For my father, Kenneth's death resulted in his standing in the local community being greatly reduced and although he maintained an outward stance of indifference, he was probably aware that some people blamed him for Kenneth's death.

I knew quite a lot of what went on at Kamilaroi because both Mum and Nicole talked to Flora about most things and she and I spoke regularly by phone. Flora told me several times that Father took his guilt and sadness out on Mum. She didn't think he'd ever hit her but he criticised her all the time. Sticking up for Nicole over Stuart seemed to be one of Father's main complaints against her. Mum was aware that Stuart could be a little Hitler and she wasn't backward in telling him what she thought of his conduct.

'You should keep out of it,' Father growled at her whenever he heard she'd remonstrated with Stuart about his treatment of Nicole. 'It's not your business what Stuart and Nicole do.'

'It *is* my business while I live at Kamilaroi. Stuart is my son and his daughters are my grandchildren. Nicole is a lovely person and I won't see her being put down and criticised. If she wasn't such a sweet woman she'd have left Stuart long ago,' said Mum, who probably didn't want Nicole to go through what she'd experienced with my father.

Underlying a lot of the friction between Stuart and Nicole was the fact that they didn't have a son to take over Kamilaroi. Neither Stuart nor my father had any faith in the ability of girls to run a place as extensive as Kamilaroi. Apparently Stuart often pressured Nicole about having another child in the hope of getting a son but she steadfastly refused.

There wasn't anything I could do to improve the general situation at home, Father and Stuart being the type of men they were. In any case, I had my own problems to deal with and they eclipsed what was happening at Kamilaroi.

When I began my career in private security, I realised that a lot of my youthful hopes had been well and truly shattered. I hadn't gone on to play big time cricket, which had been a dream of mine, and my hopes of an ideal marriage that would last all my life had gone down the drain.

After the divorce I stayed away from women, which wasn't easy since I'd always enjoyed their company. Instead I spent a lot of time practising my photography, going to classes at night in my attempt to master it. Consequently, when I wasn't at work

I was away fishing with Luke Stirling or off somewhere taking pictures.

It was a total shock when Mum rang to say that my father had died. It transpired that he'd a massive heart attack and succumbed before the ambulance could get him to hospital. The provisions of his will were just as surprising. Before he died he'd had a massive change of mind about what would happen once he passed away.

Kamilaroi had always been uppermost in Father's mind and I'm inclined to think it was the main reason he changed his will. What it all boiled down to was that he had sought to bring me home and to this effect he had ceded one third of the property and its livestock to me. Though I appreciated his decision, owning a third of Kamilaroi didn't offer sufficient inducement for me to go back. I had sworn I would never return to Kamilaroi while either Father or Stuart remained on the property and I intended to keep that oath.

I went to Father's funeral for Mum's sake, though because my private security business was still relatively new I couldn't stay away long.

Father's death made Stuart the top dog on Kamilaroi which had the effect of intensifying his high and mighty behaviour.

To escape both Stuart and the oppressive post-funeral atmosphere, I found myself drawn to the Pilliga Scrub.

As a keen amateur photographer the scrub's huge variety of wildlife had long interested me so I took the opportunity of the week after Dad's funeral to check it out. There were reputed to be at least one hundred and fifty varieties of birds in the scrub and I wanted to photograph some of them. At the top of my list was the

Red-tailed Black Cockatoo, which was a larger and noisier variety than the more plentiful Glossy Black Cockatoo. There were also persistent reports of the sighting of what might be the Red-necked Pademelon, which is a kind of small wallaby. I have never believed that there were black panthers, or even a single panther, in the Pilliga Scrub but if there is any one place such animals could be it would be the scrub because it is so vast and for much of its area so thickly covered by trees and scrub.

It was not long after I'd come back to Sydney from the week off that included Father's funeral that Mrs Eunice Kendall came to see me.

CHAPTER 6

I happened to be standing at the window contemplating my next appointment when a white Mercedes pulled into the vacant parking lot. I looked at my watch as a beautifully dressed middle-aged woman emerged from the car. Christine, my exuberant and attractive secretary, had arranged an appointment with me for a Mrs Kendall at 11am so I assumed this was the said Mrs Kendall.

Christine was the daughter of one of the grazier Baillies and had married into the Russell family, also graziers, but from what I could piece together, the marriage had been a disaster. Afterwards Christine reverted to using her maiden name and decided to accept secretarial work from Paul Ballard, a very successful financial adviser who'd gone to Scots with. When Paul offered me the adjoining suite to his own, he mentioned he had a part-time secretary who was looking for more work and asked me if I'd like to share Christine.

Christine and I got on like a house on fire from the start and she turned out to be a whizz with computers and just about everything else associated with an office. We maintained a jokey and relaxed relationship and she had a kind of sisterly concern for me. She was also very well connected, not just in tweedy country circles but in the city as well, which resulted in her bringing me a lot of well-heeled clients.

Paul and I usually had a drink together at least once a week and he'd advised me to make some investments which had turned out to be very profitable. As well as being thankful for that and for allowing me to share Christine part time I was grateful to Paul because I occupied what was probably the most up-market office of any private investigator in the business, which went over very well with clients.

From the windows of my suite in North Sydney I had a great view of the famous bridge and the Opera House. North Sydney had become a very up-market place, nothing like the dowdy and rather seedy area it used to be. In the old days North Sydney had been a dreary, uninspiring area with many narrow-fronted terrace houses and uninviting streets which were the haunt of crims. Not anymore. Our office building sat cheek by jowl with top advertising agencies and a wide variety of financial gurus.

I heard Christine talking to Mrs Kendall briefly before she showed her into my office and introduced us. My first impression was that this woman was all class. There wasn't a false note about her. Her dark hair was faultlessly set and the small, close-fitting piece of headgear she wore seemed to perfectly suit her slightly aquiline nose and dark eyes. She was wearing a dark grey beautifully tailored suit and her stockinged legs were still in good shape. Although no longer young, Eunice Kendall was still an attractive woman.

After showing her to a dark green sofa I asked Mrs Kendall if she'd like a tea or coffee.

'Nothing for the moment, Mr Sinclair. Perhaps later,' she said in a clear, well-articulated voice.

I nodded and sat down. 'How can I help you, Mrs Kendall?' I asked, sensing it would be best not to beat about the bush with this woman.

'I want you to find my daughter, Mr Sinclair,' she said.

I nodded, thinking how often I had heard that plea. Searching for missing sons and daughters comprised a not insignificant percentage of my business. The fact of the matter was that young people went missing in quite frightening numbers. Sometimes it was because they simply couldn't get on with one or both of their parents or, in the case of women, because their father or step-father (more often the latter) had sexually assaulted them – often over a long period of time. Some women went into prostitution to earn a living or finance a drug habit or help pay their way through university. If a girl really didn't want to be found she was likely to go on the game in some other state or country, which made the job of finding her even more difficult. I'd had a few such cases and assistance from the police had helped me locate some of the missing women. Then there were young people who simply disappear without trace. A few were either dumped in the bush or buried where they wouldn't be found.

'Your daughter, Mrs Kendall. How long has she been missing?' I asked.

'Just over two months,' she answered with a slight quaver in her voice.

I reached across to my desk for a pad. 'Can you please give me all her details. Her name first?' I asked.

'My daughter's name is Caroline Clemenger. She's from my first marriage, Mr Sinclair. She was taken hostage in a city bank robbery just over two months ago. Except for one piece of information there has been no other news of her,' she said.

I remembered talking to Luke Stirling about the circumstances of the robbery she was talking about. Two men had robbed an inner-city bank and had taken away a young woman who'd been in the bank when they made the heist. It had been a very audacious and well-planned raid. A third man had been waiting outside in a getaway vehicle. To the best of my knowledge the police hadn't made any headway in the case. Newspapers had reported that the men had got away with $80,000 though Luke had told me it was closer to $140,000.

'Christine recommended you to me as a man of intelligence and integrity and assured me that if anyone can find Caroline, you can. I want you to put everything else to one side so that you can concentrate on finding my daughter,' she said in a way that suggested she was used to giving orders.

I put the pad down and leaned back in my chair. 'That's asking rather a lot, Mrs Kendall. I have several other cases I'm working on. You should also understand that it's quite possible your daughter is dead.' It was a tough thing to say but I didn't want her to be under any illusions.

'I'm well aware of the possibilities, Mr Sinclair. Alive or dead, I need to know. If in fact Caroline has been murdered I want you to identify the men responsible. Either way I'm prepared to pay you whatever it takes,' she said.

'We'll come to that in a moment.' I said. 'You said you had one small piece of information. What is it, Mrs Kendall?'

'A young woman answering Caroline's description was seen sitting in a car outside a doctor's surgery in Coonabarabran,' she said, watching me closely for any reaction.

'Did you say Coonabarabran?' I said.

'I did, Mr Sinclair. I thought that would interest you,' she said.

'Was it a positive identification?' I asked.

'Positive might be too strong a word as the woman who said she saw her could have been mistaken. She thought she recognised Caroline from when they were at the same school. She wasn't aware at the time that Caroline had been abducted,' she said.

I frowned and wrote a few lines on my pad. 'How did you come by this piece of information?' I asked.

'I went to see the Commissioner of Police. It has always been my belief that if you need to know anything you go to the top of the tree to obtain it. The Commissioner was kind enough to tell me that they had information suggesting the third man in the robbery, the man who drove the getaway vehicle, comes from Coonabarabran. He did a stint in gaol for a burgling offence after which he lived at Bondi for a while though he hasn't been seen there for a couple of years. The information about the man being the driver of the getaway car came from an informant who'd heard it from someone else. The Commissioner said that it was a case that had to be handled very delicately because a heavy-handed approach by the police could have harmful consequences for Caroline,' she said.

'So, because you feel the police aren't making any progress, you want me to check out if anyone else has seen your daughter.'

'That's exactly right, Mr Sinclair.'

I shook my head. 'I can understand your concern and naturally you want to do everything in your power to find out what's happened to Caroline but this is really a police matter.'

'If you had a daughter who'd been missing for two months wouldn't you try to do something about it?' she asked.

'Yes, of course,' I said, 'but we don't know what the police are doing. They could be finding out quite a lot that you don't know about. They may well be close to cracking the case. And I absolutely agree with them about this being a case that requires delicate handling.'

'I repeat that two months is a long time, Mr Sinclair. Caroline could be dead but if she's not – and naturally I sincerely hope she isn't – the thought of her being in the hands of criminals is hard to accept. I want this matter resolved one way or the other and I want the men who abducted Caroline caught and punished,' she said.

'Tell me, what was the name of the woman who claimed to have seen your daughter?'

'Sheila Cameron,' she said and watched for my response.

'Sheila Cameron!' I exclaimed.

'Yes. Sheila went to the same school as Caroline. She was a senior when Caroline was in Year 8. Sheila is your sister-in-law, is she not?'

'Was, Mrs Kendall. Her sister and I are now divorced, so I suppose that makes Sheila my ex-sister-in-law,' I said, thinking that if it was Sheila who claimed to have seen Caroline it was very likely she did see her. But the circumstances of that sighting perplexed me. Why would crims risk discovery by parading Caroline Clemenger in the main street of Coonabarabran? It didn't make sense. There had to be a very good reason.

'What was your next move?' I asked.

'I went back to the Commissioner and he introduced me to a Superintendent Ballinger. Like Christine, both men spoke highly of you, Mr Sinclair. I am persuaded that you are my best hope of finding Caroline. I am also of the opinion that you would receive unofficial assistance from the New South Wales Police Force,' she said.

'Thank you for your confidence in my ability, Mrs Kendall. Now, would you mind answering some more questions for me?' I said. Though I was interested in the case, I hadn't yet made up my mind whether I wanted to pursue it. Even though Mrs Kendall had hinted at unofficial assistance from the NSW police I didn't want to risk treading on their toes. There hadn't been a formal demand for ransom for Caroline Clemenger so her disappearance wasn't technically a kidnapping. Not so far, anyway. If any such demand was forthcoming it would very definitely become a police matter. But the men who had abducted Caroline Clemenger were bank robbers. They'd been armed and were considered dangerous. This raised the stakes so considerably that any private detective would be reluctant to get involved single-handedly.

'I'll do anything if it means finding Caroline,' she said.

'Before I make a decision about taking this case on, I'd like to know a couple more things. Did the police tell you whether they were watching anyone in Coonabarabran or in the region gener-ally?' I asked.

'The Commissioner merely repeated what he'd told me on my first visit,' she said.

'Hmm.' It could be that the police were stepping very lightly in Coonabarabran because, given the possible sighting of Caroline

Clemenger in the main street there was a good chance the bank robbers were holed up in the area.

'Is your daughter single, married or –?' I began.

'Caroline is single,' she answered.

'Was she going out with anyone?' I asked.

'No. She didn't have one special man and she wasn't in a relationship,' she said.

'And what did she do?' I asked.

'*Do*, Mr Sinclair?' she asked with a lift of her long eyebrows.

'How did she earn her living?'

'Caroline didn't need to work. My first husband settled a great deal of money on her,' she said.

'If anything happens to her, who gets her money?' I asked.

'Most of it would come to me. We're very close, Mr Sinclair. She is a very special young woman,' she said, her voice cracking a little for the first time. 'She has many friends and is renowned for her kindness and generosity. And even though she's well placed financially she does voluntary work for the Red Cross, as well as the Children's Hospital and the Flying Doctor Service.'

I leaned back in my chair and tried to gather my thoughts. 'There are some aspects of this case I find very puzzling, Mrs Kendall. Your daughter was abducted by two, no, three men . . . bank robbers, so fairly desperate characters, and to this day nobody, most particularly you, has been contacted. If these crims are aware that your daughter is a wealthy woman with a lot of money behind her, why haven't they demanded a ransom for her?' I asked.

'How would they know she's wealthy?' Mrs Kendall asked.

I looked at the rings on her fingers, her gold wristlet watch and her gold necklace and brooch. 'Was your daughter wearing much jewellery that day?' I asked.

'Caroline always wore *some* jewellery, Mr Sinclair,' she said.

'What would it have been worth? Ten thousand? Fifteen thousand?' I asked.

'Possible a bit more than that,' she said.

'So she would have presented as a wealthy young woman. They'd have taken her jewellery but why haven't they asked for money for her?' I asked.

'They may not have connected Caroline to me. They'd have looked through her handbag and found that her name is Clemenger, not Kendall,' she said.

I had the first stirrings in my mind of an outrageous thought. 'That would suggest that your daughter hasn't let on that you're her mother or you would have been contacted by now,' I said. 'Let me bounce a thought off you. It's wild but it might just fit the situation. It seems to me that there's a strong possibility that your daughter has either lost her memory or has been able to convince her abductors that she has.'

Her eyes widened and I detected a gleam in them for the first time. 'That is a very interesting suggestion, Mr Sinclair. Such a possibility hadn't occurred to me but perhaps you're right.'

'It's only conjecture at this stage because I'm grasping at straws. Let us suppose that these bank robbers believe that Caroline is from a moneyed family. One reason that you haven't been contacted could be because your daughter is playing a very cool game. She is either acting as if she's suffered memory loss or is actually suffering from such a loss,' I said.

'Why do you say that?' she asked.

'If I remember correctly, the newspaper report on the robbery said that the female hostage had hit her head when she was pulled through the bank's front door and one of the robbers caught her and threw her over his shoulder.' I thanked the Lord for my police training because it was remembering things like that which often made the difference between success and failure. Nobody could hope to be a really good detective, a top detective, unless he or she had a good memory for details.

'Very impressive, Mr Sinclair,' she said.

'It seems to me that we are faced with three possibilities. Assuming it was Caroline who was sighted in Coonabarabran – which I believe is probable given the witness was Sheila Cameron – the worst case scenario is that your daughter has been murdered and is buried somewhere in the vastness of the Pilliga Scrub. The Pilliga is over a million acres so the chances of locating her body are remote. The second possibility is that your daughter is being held for sex. Three men holed up with a young woman. It's not a pretty picture. Have you considered that possibility?' I asked.

'Constantly, Mr Sinclair. I'm well aware of how men behave,' she said. 'I get very little sleep thinking of all the things that could have happened or be happening to her.'

'Of course. The third possibility is that the people holding her will seek a ransom. We've established that Caroline was wearing expensive jewellery and that might be why the kidnappers chose her rather than any of the bank's other clients who were there at the time. The jewellery might just be the saving of her, Mrs Kendall. It all depends on the calibre of the crims who abducted her,' I said.

'Calibre, Mr Sinclair?' said Mrs Kendall frostily.

'Even among the criminal fraternity there are degrees of behaviour, Mrs Kendall. What I mean by calibre is that some crooks won't do certain things. For example, some crooks would never harm a woman. Armed robbery is a very serious crime and it can attract a considerable term in gaol. If it's compounded with rape it becomes a seriously nasty offence and under certain circumstances it can attract a life sentence. In the very worst cases, the offenders may never be released. What I'm saying is that there are crims, and plenty of them, who wouldn't baulk at armed robbery but would never contemplate either rape or murder, so Caroline's fate may rest in the hands of whoever is in charge of the robbers. If he's purely a bank robber and if he exerts a strong influence over his associates, your daughter could be held in comparatively reasonable surroundings.'

'You are an impressive man, Mr Sinclair. Will you help me? I assure you I will make it well worth your while,' she said.

'Would you like a cup of tea?' I asked, wanting more time to make a decision.

'I'd prefer a glass of water,' she said.

I called for Christine to bring some water for Mrs Kendall and a cup of coffee for me. Mrs Kendall drank half a glass of the water and then looked at me expectantly.

'How would you describe your daughter, Mrs Kendall?' I asked.

'I don't understand your question, Mr Sinclair,' she said with a frown.

'What kind of person is she? Would you say she's smart enough to try and pull the wool over the eyes of the men who've kidnapped her? Has she got enough nerve to do that or would she go to pieces very quickly?' I asked.

'Caroline is no spoilt brat. She's a very strong-minded person. She's trekked in Nepal and photographed big game in Africa and she trades on the stock exchange. She can sail a boat, has fished for marlin, skis well and rides a horse beautifully,' she said.

'And would you describe your daughter as being a resourceful person?'

'Resourceful?' she said and thought about it for a while.

'I think I could truthfully describe Caroline as resourceful. She has been in a few tight situations and weathered them well. She's quite adventurous. What are you trying to establish, Mr Sinclair?' she asked.

'What I'm trying to establish is whether your daughter might perhaps be playing a game with her abductors. This is to support my theory, and I stress that it's only a theory, that the reason neither you nor anyone else has had any word about Caroline is because the men who are holding her don't know who she is. And maybe that's because Caroline hasn't told them,' I said.

I could see that she was about to say something but I hadn't finished so I put up my hand to stop her.

'Let me bounce this scenario off you, Mrs Kendall. They got Caroline into the getaway vehicle and they probably intended to dump her when they got clear of the city. But one of those three robbers was cluey enough to realise that the jewellery Caroline was wearing was worth big bikkies which probably meant that she had serious money behind her. They'd have been discussing what to do with her and maybe Caroline was half-conscious and heard them.

If she's the kind of woman you tell me she is, she'd have realised that her best chance of surviving would be to kid them that she'd lost her memory. She'd have to be quite resourceful to pull it off but I dare say it could be done. And maybe the reason the crims took her to Coonabarabran that day was to check out how she'd behave. If she'd tried to escape they probably would have done for her. But that's pure conjecture and there might have been some other reason,' I said.

Mrs Kendall leaned back in her chair and actually smiled at me. 'I feel a great deal better already, Mr Sinclair. Now, will you help me?'

I looked across at the big pastoral map above my desk. It was a very large blow-up of the Pilliga Scrub from east to west and from north to south. 'If your daughter is being held by Coonabarabran-based crims then it's a safe bet that she and they are tucked away somewhere in the Pilliga Scrub. There are a million acres in the Pilliga and it could take me a long time to track her down. And then again I might never find her. I couldn't give you any guarantee of success. I'd need a four-wheel drive vehicle and would have to camp out for days at a time,' I said bluntly.

'I would be most grateful for a quick resolution. You do know the area well, don't you? You were reared there and your people have a large property close to the Pilliga Scrub?' This was as much a statement as a question. It was already clear she'd done some research on me.

I nodded my agreement. 'It's because I know the Pilliga Scrub and the general Coonabarabran area reasonably well that I'm aware how big a job this could turn out to be.' I said, doing some rapid calculations about on-going cases, including which ones could be handled by someone else plus what fee I could reasonably charge on a weekly basis.

My first thought of who might take over while I was away was Dasher Doyle, a retired ex-detective sergeant out of police records whom I'd used quite often to dig out information on a variety of matters. Inside three months from retiring Dasher had been bored to tears because of the amount of time he suddenly had on his hands. I'd bumped into him one day at the Sydney Cricket Ground and we'd had a yarn about a lot of things. The upshot of this chance meeting was that I'd offered Dasher some part-time work. He grabbed at the offer like a blackfish biting at green weed. Since then he'd worked on several cases with me and been a real asset. In typically Australian fashion he'd been given the nickname Dasher because he was anything but. However, he would stick at a problem and not let up until he solved it.

'So you'll take the case?' she pressed.

'I'll take the case subject to certain conditions. And let me say at the outset that we have to use our heads, Mrs Kendall. Above all else we need to be secretive. One hint that there's someone on their scent and those crims could decide to get rid of Caroline. She's a witness to what they've done, which is probably why the police are treading so lightly,' I said.

'My feeling is that sooner or later these men will give themselves away. I'm convinced that you're the man to find them when they do,' Mrs Kendall said firmly.

'Occasionally, very occasionally, you strike a smart crim who doesn't follow the usual pattern of criminal behaviour. He doesn't gravitate to the Gold Coast or the Cross. He or she will lie low until the hue and cry about the crime dies down. But smart or otherwise there's usually a weak spot. Find this and it'll eventually lead you to them. There aren't many really successful crims,' I said.

Mrs Kendall nodded.

'There's also the fact that men don't rob banks so they can hide away forever. Not many men can take being holed up for long . . .'

I looked at my map again and tried to imagine what it would be like to camp out in the Pilliga once more . . . no traffic, no hassles and some more time to devote to photographing the area.

She noted my hesitation and tried another tack. 'Is there something holding you back from going? Someone?'

I shook my head. 'I've said that I'll take the case but it's only fair that I tell you that it could cost you a lot of money and it could be money down the drain. I don't like taking money from clients unless I believe there's a reasonable chance I can deliver the goods. I can't give you an unequivocal guarantee about that and it would be unethical for me to try. The police haven't been able to either identify or locate these crims and their resources are far greater than mine. There's also the fact that I would have to work closely with the police and they'd have to be willing to cooperate. Speaking generally, the police don't welcome outsiders. They welcome information from the public but not active participation by members of the public. I'd have to go armed and be ready for anything. If I went up against those men on my own there'd be a good chance that they'd shoot me and your daughter. I'll need back-up and that means the police. They can't stop me from making enquiries about the whereabouts of your daughter but they'd be justifiably concerned if this affects in any way their attempts to apprehend the bank robbers who abducted her,' I explained.

'I have reason to believe that the police will be willing to cooperate. If you have any trouble in that regard, let me know. I can muster quite a lot of influence, Mr Sinclair. Now, just tell me what you require,' she said.

'Like I told you, I'll need a four-wheel drive vehicle and more camping gear than I currently have,' I said.

She waved her hand in front of her face as if to signify that the cost of buying a vehicle was unimportant. 'Keep going, Mr Sinclair. What else do you require?' she asked.

I did some rapid financial calculations to cover what I'd have to pay Dasher Doyle and Christine plus the lease of the suite and some provision for motels because I wouldn't be camping out every night.

'Four thousand dollars a week and if it takes longer than a month, three thousand dollars a week,' I said.

She took a cheque book from her handbag and wrote out a cheque which she handed to me. The cheque was for $16,000. 'There's your first four weeks' payment beginning from today,' she said.

I put the cheque in my pocket and smiled across at her. 'It seems that I'm headed for the Pilliga,' I said.

'I didn't add the money for the vehicle because I'll have someone attend to that. We have accounts with a couple of the major vehicle distributors and I'll get a better deal than you. You can have the vehicle as soon as you like.'

'Okay, but don't buy the vehicle in my name, Mrs Kendall. Buy it in one of your company names. We don't want my name connected to the vehicle,' I said.

'I understand,' she said. 'And if you find my daughter the vehicle will be yours to keep. I'll have a legal document drawn up by my solicitors and delivered to this office as soon as is physically possible. If you locate my daughter alive I'll pay you two hundred and fifty thousand dollars. If she's been murdered and you can identify the men who killed her, I'll pay you the same amount. Is that satisfactory?' she asked.

The money she was offering was exceedingly generous. It and the vehicle amounted to about three hundred thousand dollars but I'd be going up against bank robbers so there was always the chance that I wouldn't live to earn it.

'The money you're offering is very generous, Mrs Kendall. The worst case scenario is that I get killed but that was also a possibility when I was a detective. The second worst case scenario is that these creeps have killed your daughter and that although I might identify them, there wouldn't be sufficient evidence to charge them. Or they could be charged and subsequently acquitted,' I said.

'I'll take that risk. So we have a deal?' she said.

Any way I looked at it her offer was too good to turn down. 'We have a deal,' I agreed and shook hands with her. 'Just one more thing. How long do I go on looking for Caroline?'

'Until you've exhausted every avenue, Mr Sinclair,' she said, smiling warmly. Under her classy exterior and business-like manner she seemed like an all right woman. 'You've taken a big load off my mind and I might even get some sleep tonight knowing that the search for Caroline is in as good hands as it can possibly be. It's been terrible to feel so useless.'

'Do you have a good photograph of Caroline?' I asked.

She nodded before delving into her handbag and taking out a large mauve envelope, which she handed to me. I slipped out three photographs and spread them out on my desk. The face I was looking at was not one I was likely to forget in a hurry. Though Caroline Clemenger wasn't as beautiful as Sheila Cameron nor was her face as classically etched as Fiona's it was full of character. Caroline was a handsome young woman with a wealth of dark, glossy hair. The expression on her face suggested a woman who was ready to take on the world and conceivably do almost anything, including outwitting a trio of bank robbers. The thought of such a woman in the hands of crims made me see red and I hoped she was everything her mother claimed her to be and capable of coping with her abductors.

'May I keep these? I can have copies made if you want them back,' I said.

She waved an elegant hand and I got another squiz of the rings she was wearing. Lord knows what they were worth. If Caroline had been wearing rings of similar quality, plus other jewellery, this cornucopia of riches provided ample reason for holding her.

'They are copies, Mr Sinclair. I came prepared. The Commissioner and Superintendent Ballinger warned me that you'd require photographs. I've had several long conversations with both men and I'm assured that the police will help you in every way possible,' she said. 'And as I've already hinted, I have good contacts at high levels and will do everything to ensure continued cooperation with you from the police.'

Now I had quite often had help from the police and I had just as often helped them with information but I had never before been given such a positive message of police cooperation. It wasn't that Mrs Kendall wouldn't be quite equal to holding her own with the Commissioner and Ballinger or anyone else in the country. There was only one element that would bring so much weight to bear on the police that they would be willing to offer such cooperation: that was influence. How high it went I didn't know but I suspected that it would be coming from the police minister.

'I think I have everything I need,' I said. 'Do you have any more questions?' I asked.

'Only one. When can you leave?' she asked.

I looked up at the calendar and did some quick figuring. 'I have a few things here I really have to either organise or finalise. You must appreciate that I can't go racing off to the Pilliga without any preparation. I'll need to look at what I might describe as the active list of villains, see who's locked up and who isn't. That might not tell us a lot because the police reckon the men who took your daughter are new boys on the job. But I'll have a look anyway. Then there's the matter of the vehicle and the camping gear. I'll leave as soon as you can get those to me.'

'If you tell me the make of vehicle you'd prefer and give me a list of your other requirements, I'll get onto them straight away. I'm very anxious for you to make a start,' she said.

I scribbled out a list of my requirements and handed the page to her. She glanced at the list and then stowed it away in her handbag. 'If you think of anything else you need please tell Christine to let me know. Will you send me progress reports?' she asked.

'Definitely not,' I said firmly. 'You'll only hear from me when I've got something concrete to report. You can get in touch with me via Christine,' I said. 'One final word of caution. Don't discuss the fact that I'm working for you with *anyone*. Not a word. What we have discussed in this office must remain confidential to the two of us. The media must not get a whiff of *anything* because if it gets out it could mean your daughter's life.'

'I understand,' she said. 'And thank you.'

She held out her hand and I shook it. 'I'll do all I can to locate your daughter, Mrs Kendall.'

'I have a great deal of confidence in you, Mr Sinclair,' she said, tears in her eyes.

After seeing her out I went back to my office and called Christine in. I told her that I'd be going bush within the week and I would greatly appreciate it if she could look after everything in my absence. 'This case might take months or I could get lucky and nail it down fairly quickly,' I told her. 'And I'm thinking I'll get Dasher Doyle in to run things until I get back. You don't have any problems working with Dasher, do you?' I asked.

'Not really. He's not a bad old sod when you get used to him,' she said giving me a cheeky grin.

'When will you leave?' Christine asked.

'More or less when Mrs Kendall can get the vehicle and camping gear to me,' I said. 'Naturally, she's very anxious for me to make a start. I'll need to get Dasher to do some preliminary checking of potential suspects for me. Superintendent Ballinger might help me with those,' I said.

'What do I tell people when they ask where you are?' she said.

'You can tell them I'm away working on a very important case in New Zealand and am temporarily incommunicado. But not a word to anyone about who I'm working for or where I actually am. You'll know, Dasher will know and Luke will know. Also, it turns out that Mrs Kendall has very good connections with the Commissioner and Ballinger, so they'll know too,' I said.

'Okay big chief, I better get on with organising things,' she said and left the office as I sat down to ring Dasher Doyle.

CHAPTER 7

I resolved to get Dasher Doyle working full bore on preliminary aspects of the Kendall case but before I could get him properly started I had to meet with Luke. Since leaving the force we'd bought a small half cabin launch together and we spent many enjoyable hours out fishing on the water. Luke and I could sit in a boat with our eyes on floats and not say a word for half an hour and be perfectly content. We had a competition going for the heaviest fish of its variety. I was ahead of Luke in flathead, bream and black-fish (luderick) but Luke was on top with mulloway, snapper and trevally.

Working with Luke had been one of the best experiences of my life. Tall and slim with blue eyes that could be full of laughter, Luke had a very dry sense of humour and often used it in tight situations. When we were working on a case we'd analyse it from go to whoa so each of us knew it backward. Luke was a very cool fellow and often applied the brakes if I appeared to be going into overdrive. It was through being teamed with him that I'd become a better detective because he'd showed me how to think. He had earned a lot of respect and I was always confident that he'd go on to big things.

Unlike me, Luke was a career police officer.

I debated meeting Luke at our usual watering hole but what I wanted to discuss with him was too sensitive to air in a public place, so I asked him to come to my office.

'What's the current drill on the unsolved bank job?' I asked after he'd arrived and Christine had brought us coffee and cake.

'What's it to you?' he asked, still a bit peeved about missing out on his beer and having to settle for coffee. My use of the word 'unsolved' may also have touched a raw nerve since the police appeared to have made no headway on this case. He was a real pro and like all good police officers, unsolved cases were like a red rag to a bull.

'Let's just say that my question is on a need-to-know basis,' I said.

'Have you been retained by the bank?' he asked. This would be really rubbing salt into the wound.

I shook my head.

'Mrs Kendall?'

'Got it in two,' I said.

'There's not much I can tell you, Lachie. We know that there were three men involved. One drove the getaway car and we got a reasonable description of him but it could fit a thousand men. The other two were wearing balaclavas. We think these same two men did two earlier, smaller heists. The whisper is that they could be from the bush.'

'Is that so?' I said, trying not to give anything away.

'I haven't been involved so I can't tell you a lot,' said Luke. There was a limit to what he would tell me now I wasn't a cop because Luke was a very ethical fellow.

'Do you reckon I could get hold of an up-to-date list of all hold-up types, local and interstate?' I asked.

'It might be possible,' Luke said, giving me a keen look. 'I'll ask the super. He might be prepared to do a deal.'

I wasn't concerned about doing a deal because I realised I couldn't handle this case on my own. If I located the crims who'd pulled the bank job, the police were welcome to them. Caroline Clemenger was my priority.

Sure enough I received a message stating that Superintendent Ballinger wished to see me and we made an appointment to meet at 2 p.m. the next day.

As a female police constable shepherded me through to Ballinger's office I got a few curious looks but there was nobody there I recognised from the past. It had been a few years and most of the old hands were bound to have moved on or up. Ballinger stood up and walked towards me, a half smile on his face which boded well for the meeting. He was greyer now than when I'd last seen him but he was still the same Ballinger, the personification of everything that was best about the police force; incorruptible, committed to fighting crime and a man whose word was his bond.

'You're looking well, Lachie,' he said as we shook hands.

'I still exercise a lot and I've kept my eye in with firearms,' I said.

He nodded. Luke probably kept him fairly well informed about my activities. And Ballinger had a brain that absorbed information like a sponge and he never forgot a thing.

'You've done fairly well, I hear,' he said.

'I'm not complaining, Super,' I said.

'So now you've been retained by Mrs Kendall to try and find her daughter which we haven't been able to do,' he said dryly.

'That's right, Super. I hope you'll look kindly on my efforts,' I said. 'I appreciate that the matter will require delicate handling given the missing woman may still be in the hands of the bank robbers.'

Ballinger nodded and gave me a précis of the situation as he knew it which included references to Mrs Kendall's meetings with the Commissioner and himself. He admitted quite candidly that they hadn't made much progress in the case beyond having some ideas about the identity of the driver of the getaway car. They had been concerned that if they went looking for him it might put Caroline Clemenger's life at risk if she was still alive. They'd been hoping some word would come from her abductors.

'I suppose Mrs Kendall told you that there was supposed to have been a sighting of Caroline Clemenger in a car in the main street of Coonabarabran,' I said.

'Yes, but I wouldn't put a lot of faith in it, Lachie. Why would crims risk detection by parading Miss Clemenger in the main street of a smallish town? It doesn't make sense,' said Ballinger.

'Maybe it doesn't, except that according to what Mrs Kendall told me it was Sheila Cameron who claimed she saw Caroline Clemenger sitting in the car outside the doctor's surgery. I know Sheila and she's very trustworthy and she also went to the same school as Caroline Clemenger and had seen pictures of Caroline as an adult in magazines. Sheila was fairly positive it was Caroline Clemenger, though she didn't know at the time that Caroline had been abducted,' I said.

'It places us in a difficult situation, Lachie. We have a good idea that the bloke who drove the getaway car is a bloke by the name of Ted Challis. He did a stint in gaol and after that he had a flat at Bondi for a while but he hasn't been seen there for a couple of years. He hasn't been seen in Coonabarabran either, which suggests he's keeping a very low profile and that the other two are going out for supplies. It might also suggest that they're planning another bank job but that's pure speculation on my part. As you know, we've been careful about not asking a lot of questions, in case we scare them off. We haven't anything concrete to go on. My personal feeling is that Caroline Clemenger is probably dead. She'd be a material witness to the bank heist. And if they abducted her with the idea of demanding money for her, why haven't they contacted anyone?' said Ballinger.

I bounced my loss of memory theory off him or that Caroline Clemenger might be faking loss of memory. I wanted to give him something before I left his office because I was going to be asking a lot from him.

'That's a fair enough theory, Lachie, but I still think she's more likely to be dead. If we were sure about it, we could risk raiding a few places, but we aren't and we can't. They could be using her for sex. Three crims holed up with a lot of time on their hands. How many blokes would keep a young woman for two months unless they were getting something from her?' he said.

Though everything he said made sense, and there was nobody who knew crims better than Ballinger, I had the feeling that Caroline Clemenger was alive and I intended to proceed on that assumption.

'You could be right, Super, but I'm rather keen on my memory loss theory.' And then I told him about all the expensive jewellery Caroline had been wearing the day of the bank robbery. It might have been worth as much as twenty thousand. 'The crims couldn't contact anyone in her family if she couldn't remember who she is or is pretending she can't,' I said.

Ballinger looked at me for a few moments while he tossed my theory around in his head. 'You're still pretty sharp, Lachie,' he said at last.

'I hope I'm sharp enough to locate Caroline Clemenger so that you guys can nail this bunch,' I said.

'Well if anyone can do it, you can,' he said. 'And I hope you can, Lachie, because there's a lot of pressure on us about this and I could be posted to Bullamakanka if we make a hash of it,' he said grimly.

'I wouldn't have thought that God could shift *you* to Bullama-kanka,' I said.

'Let's get down to tin tacks, Lachie. I'll give you the list you asked for but don't trumpet that around,' he said. 'Now, how do you propose to work things?'

'I'll be posing as a wildlife photographer. I've got all the gear, or will have by the time I leave, even a hide. I'll look the genuine article because I'll be the genuine article. I've been studying photography and taking pictures ever since Fiona and I broke up,' I said.

'That could be just the dodge, Lachie. But be careful. There are three blokes all of whom are likely to be armed and you're just one man alone in the bush, it's risky,' he said.

'Taking someone else up there would be a dead giveaway, Super. Two men wouldn't get within a bull's roar of these blokes, always providing they're up in that area,' I said.

'I agree but I still think that what you're taking on is very risky. Granted that you know the area fairly well but that doesn't detract from the fact that one man camped out in the bush is very vulnerable,' Ballinger said gravely.

'That's where you might be able to help me, Super. If I can locate these creeps how would you feel about sending me up a smart policewoman who could pose as my girlfriend,' I said.

Ballinger looked at me as if he thought I'd taken temporary leave of my senses. 'I doubt very much that the Commissioner would agree to that,' he said.

'It wouldn't be any different to her working undercover,' I said.

'It would because you're not a police officer. If you were still a cop, it would be a different matter. But we couldn't order a female policewoman to do the job, she'd have to volunteer,' said Ballinger.

'I could always ask Mrs Kendall to use her influence,' I said.

'Hold your horses, Lachie. This is not a proposal I can decide here and now,' said Ballinger.

'The situation may not arise at all but I need to know now what cooperation I can get if things heat up. If I locate these creeps you can have them and all the credit. I'm really only interested in Caroline Clemenger,' I said.

'Speaking of cooperation, you'll have all the local resources. Do you want me to ring Coonabarabran and let them know you're on the way?' Ballinger asked.

'No, I don't want you to do that, Super. I want to bowl in there and see what sort of reception I get. It would give me a good idea of what I could expect from the local cops. Their chief would need to clear it with their sub-district who'd probably get in touch with you,' I said.

'That's right,' Ballinger agreed.

'I'll keep you informed. If you need to contact me, fax me at Coonabarabran police station [or email me at lr@bigpond.com]. I'm going to use Rivers as my surname.'

'Watch your step, Lachie. The last time I told you that was just before you got shot,' said Ballinger.

'I will, Super. By the way, how is Alison these days?' I asked.

'She's good. She's still single and working at the Children's Hospital,' said Ballinger. 'When I retire I want to move up to Port Macquarie or Coffs Harbour and she's said she'd probably set up there when I do.'

'So when are you going to retire?' I asked.

'There are some cases I want to wrap up before I leave. It's a matter of finishing the job on the right note,' said Ballinger.

'Nobody could accuse you of not finishing the job on the right note. The only way you could finish any better is as Commissioner,' I said.

'I don't want to be Commissioner. I just want to be able to get away from Sydney and move up the coast so I can go out in my boat and fish. I've had a lifetime of dealing with crims and I've had enough,' said Ballinger.

'I should think you have. Can you give me a picture of Ted Challis?' I asked.

'I think we could manage that. I'll have Luke deliver it to you with the list of names you've asked for,' said Ballinger.

'Thanks, Super. I'll keep you posted,' I said.

I left Police Headquarters fairly satisfied, all things considered. I'd been promised the list I'd requested and I'd got the promise, unofficially of course, of police back-up. I hadn't received an unequivocal promise that they'd send me a policewoman if I requested one but I'd sown the seeds and I might yet get her.

Luke delivered the list I'd requested in person early the next morning. Half an hour later I sat Dasher down and handed him the list. 'I want you to compile every known fact about the crims on this list. I especially want to know where they were born and where they grew up. I want to know who's locked up and who isn't. The first person I want to know about is this fellow, Ted Challis,' I said and stabbed my finger against the last name on the list. This was the fellow suspected of having driven the getaway vehicle. The police hadn't got him in for questioning because they couldn't lay their hands on him and they didn't want to endanger Caroline Clemenger in the process of trying to find him.

I didn't know much about the Challis family beyond the fact that my father had never given any member of that family the time of day. I had had no contact with any of them.

Dasher worked well into the night and in ways known only to him, which I'm sure involved some police connivance, the information I'd requested was on my desk when I arrived early the next morning. Ted Challis, the fellow suspected of being the third man in the bank robbery, had definitely been born in Coonabarabran. He'd done some time for burglary and was believed to have been involved in a couple of hold-ups but minor stuff really. He'd also been involved with car racing though he'd never been a Jack Brabham.

It wasn't a bad start, though the names of the other crims on the list who might provide clues about the identity of the other two men didn't give me any help. Most of the listed men were serving time and the couple that weren't didn't come across as big-time bank robbers. The only conclusion I could draw was that the fellows who had done the bank job and abducted Caroline Clemenger were new men, which was the police view. Certainly, they hadn't been able to lift any fingerprints of known criminals.

'Nice going, Dasher,' I said when he came into the office. 'Will you put everything you've got on disc? It might come in very handy,' I said.

He gave me a sour look. 'As if I wouldn't put it on a disc,' he growled, his mood probably affected by a wife nagging at him for staying up so late while he worked on my list.

'Sorry Dasher, there's a lot riding on this case,' I said.

'So Christine told me,' he said. Christine was his shining star. 'Any of that stuff useful?'

'Probably more than I can imagine at the moment. I'll leave you to look after everything for now. I have to go and check out a vehicle,' I told him.

Mrs Kendall had moved incredibly fast on leasing my vehicle and had rung and asked Christine where the four-wheel drive should be delivered. I'd told her to have it delivered to my house at Neutral Bay. Between them they'd arranged for the vehicle and everything else I'd asked for to be delivered between 11 a.m. and noon and it was. Mrs Kendall was clearly eager for me to leave as soon as possible.

Having a four-wheel drive would be crucial because there were many sandy tracks and sandy creek crossings in the Pilliga Scrub. When a lot of rain fell it could shift tonnes of sand and you could get bogged very easily. I'd been pulled out of such places so I knew the drill. I was planning to camp out as much as possible. There was also the fact that the more I camped out, the more opportunities I would have to take some great pictures.

One of the last things I did was to purchase the 400-mm lens I'd been promising myself for some time. The longest lens I had was a 300 mm which was a really superb lens but not up to the 400 mm for long distance wildlife photography, especially for birds. This lens cost a lot of money but with the promise of an assured income for some time, I felt confident buying it as well as another tripod.

I went back to the office, looked over the information Dasher had dug up for me and spent some time going over my current cases with him.

I had a farewell drink with Luke Stirling that evening and told him I'd be leaving Sydney early the next morning.

'I might be away for a while,' I told him. 'On the other hand I might get lucky and it won't take long.'

'You be bloody careful, Lachie,' he cautioned me. 'This might not be a picnic. Being a one-man band isn't the same as having a reliable partner or a back-up squad behind you. And I'm aware of how you operate.'

I told him I'd have the local police to call on should I need them.

'It isn't the same as having another cop beside you,' he said.

'Granted, but you can't have everything in life,' I said.

'Mrs Kendall might be paying you a lot of money, but it'll be no good to you if you're dead,' he said.

'If anything should happen to me you know what to do,' I said. After my father's death I'd changed my will and named Luke as my executor. 'You get the boat. In the meantime, good fishing.'

'You too, Lachie. And if you need a hand I'll ask the Super if he'll allow me to join you,' Luke said with a grin.

I knew he would too.

Soon after, we parted company. As I waved goodbye to Luke I thought how Judy was the kind of wife I would have liked to have. She was a bottler of a woman and I was very fond of her. Luke's home life was everything I had ever wanted and hoped for, with two great kids and a settled marriage.

Quite above and beyond the financial aspects of this case there were some unrelated plusses to be gained from this trip. I'd see Mum again and I'd also see Flora and Laurie and their two wonderful kids. It'd be great to see Sheila again too, quite apart from her being the person who'd seen Caroline Clemenger after her abduction. There had to be more to that story than I had heard so far.

I was ready to leave Sydney and head for the Pilliga Scrub, that vast and unique region that had seemed so magical and mysterious to me as a kid. I reckoned I was probably facing the biggest challenge of my life. Win or lose, the next few weeks, or months, were going to be very interesting. If I was successful, I would be much better off financially. If I wasn't, well, I might not be coming home.

First things first though. I had to try and get a sniff of the bank robbers. They might be in the Pilliga or they might not. The only lead I
had suggested that they were more likely to be there than anywhere
else. But the only way to make any progress was to be on the spot.

CHAPTER 8

I got up early, wanting to get clear of Sydney before the morning rush hour. It wasn't long before I got to the freeway and then I drove north through Wyee, Calga and Cessnock before picking up the New England Highway at Branxton. After stopping for an early lunch at Merriwa's classic small-town Greek café, I set off again. It felt good to be escaping Sydney – I was still a country boy at heart.

Driving past the iconic old Collaroy Station, one of Australia's earliest merino studs, I remembered being told about some leg irons being unearthed there, relics of the days when convicts were allocated to owners of properties. Having crossed the Castlereagh River at Binnaway I re-crossed it some distance down the road towards Coonabarabran, and before long I was, to use an old bush saying, within a bull's roar of the southern extremity of the Pilliga Scrub.

The proximity of the scrub was signalled by the appearance of scattered groups of cypress pines and the changing colour of the ground beside the road. It was a kind of reddish-yellow. There'd been a shower the previous day which accentuated the characteristic bush odour familiar to anyone who'd lived in the Pilliga region. A combination of wet earth and pine scent, it brought back lots of memories.

Not long after I crossed the river for the second time, I slowed down and started looking for a place to sleep overnight while there was still plenty of daylight. As well as wanting to try out my new 400-mm lens before it got dark, I wanted to have completely set up camp before sundown. Only a new chum makes camp after dark in the Australian bush because it's so important to inspect the surrounding area in order to avoid sharing your tent with dangerous snakes, ants whose sting is pure agony and numerous other venomous creatures.

After pulling in off the road I soon found what appeared to be a good site. There were no ant's nests close by and no fallen logs. And only minutes away there was plenty of firewood scattered about. Before long I had my tent up, a fire going and the billy on. It was clear as I unpacked my collapsible table, chair and cutlery that Eunice Kendall hadn't spared any expense with the camping equipment.

There was a crow pecking at something beside the road perhaps fifty metres away and I focused my new 400-mm lens on it. The result was overwhelming so I took a couple of pictures of it, feeling very happy.

Sitting in my chair after an early dinner, I contemplated the nearby road that led to Coonabarabran. I was back in the country of my childhood. Ahead of me were the Warrumbungles with all their timeless mystery. They had been here untold years before the first human, black or white, arrived in this region. They had witnessed the first comings of indigenous people and the passing of the tribal way of life.

Estimates of how long people had lived in this region ranged from 7500 to 25,000 years. Kamilaroi was the name used to describe the tribes and sub-tribes who occupied a vast area of northern New South Wales. Kamilaroi country extended from Murrurundi in the south, Mungindi in the north and almost as far as Brewarrina in the north-west. The term Kamilaroi was also used to describe all the tribes who spoke the Gamilaraay language. The Kamilaroi people had traditionally occupied the eastern side of the Castlereagh River and the Mole tribe of the Wiradjuri the western side.

Australia's rivers had naturally been a magnet for indigenous people as a source of not just water but food, since animals also came to them to drink. The Kamilaroi people would have fished in the Castlereagh River as well as hunting other animals, principally kangaroos. Anything that walked or crawled was utilised for food.

Life changed dramatically for the Kamilaroi people when white squatters moved into the area in the 1830s. Whereas the resources of the region had hitherto been ample for them, with the arrival of the white fella food sources were soon stretched. Kamilaroi men were shot at and their women abducted by white stockmen. After the retaliatory murder of a white settler by the Kamilaroi in the Warrumbungle district, punitive expeditions by mounted police resulted in widespread death amongst the tribes with 50 aborigines killed on one such expedition. Even more devastating to the Kamilaroi people were white fella diseases like smallpox, which cut a swathe through their numbers. With such widespread death, much of the knowledge of the local culture had vanished.

Dragging my thoughts away from the past to the present, I decided to try out the new powerful radio Mrs Kendall had supplied, switching it on just before the 7 p.m. news on the ABC. The reception wasn't at all bad though there was nothing of much importance reported so, tired after a day's travelling, I decided to have an early night. Mrs Kendall had been extremely generous in her understanding of my camping needs. I hadn't asked for a radio because there was a good radio in the vehicle, but she'd supplied a great set. Likewise, all the camping gear was of the very highest quality.

I had a swag and a separate pillow, which I put my Browning pistol beneath. I had a Mannlicher rifle and a 12-gauge shotgun in a case beside me, though it was technically illegal to transport firearms in a vehicle. A phone call to Ballinger would fix that. I also had the most up-to-date mobile phone.

It took me only a few minutes to drop off, and whether it was the change of air or the solitude and scarcity of vehicles, or just feeling more comfortable in the country I'd grown up in, I had a great night's sleep.

I woke feeling on top of the world. It was a cool, fresh morning, harbinger of a great day. After I'd finished cooking and eating a hearty breakfast I had a second mug of tea. As I was drinking my tea, a truck laden with cypress logs slugged past my camp, its driver waving to me in typical bush fashion. I smiled and waved back – suddenly it was as if I'd never left the bush. I could feel myself slipping back into my old world, in which the accent was on weather and seasons, stock and grain prices and the annual show.

After my tea I savoured the peace around me. For much of its area the Pilliga Scrub is thicker than it was when the first white man arrived in the area. In those days it was open savannah-like country with the growth of saplings and scrub kept in check by annual fires, which the Kamilaroi used to flush out game. Such was the intensity of vegetation now that a person could quite easily get lost in some areas of the scrub. Even competent bushmen had been known to take a compass into the Pilliga when they searched for new timber sites.

It was only just after six but I was keen to get on my way, conscious that if Caroline Clemenger was still alive, every day she was held hostage would be agony for her. Before I did so I wanted to spend a bit more time thinking about how to proceed. As I started to pack up, a white police car with two men in the front seat flashed past me travelling south, the passenger turning his head sharply to get a squiz at me as they shot past. A few minutes later an ambulance tore down the road in the wake of the police car.

Presently a tow truck appeared from the direction of Coonabarabran. As its driver – a youngish fellow – gave me the usual bush wave, I noticed the graphic on the door was that of the garage my father used to deal with. I hoped he hadn't recognised me. The possibility that there'd been a bad accident got me thinking about Kenneth's death. Even after all these years, I'd never really come to terms with him dying so tragically, his so very promising life cut short.

The only thing to do now before I set off was pack up my photography equipment. Just as I was about to do so, the ambulance from before returned at a great rate of knots, siren blaring, followed closely by the white police car. To my surprise, as the police car neared my vehicle it slowed, turned off the road and pulled to a stop almost beside me. Two constables, both well built fellows, one a two-striper, got out of the car and came towards me. The younger of the two looked keenly at my camera set-up. A 400-mm lens mounted on a tripod wasn't the kind of thing a country cop would see very often I supposed. Certainly not beside a road.

'Bad accident?' I asked and nodded towards the south.

'Bloody idiots. Some fellas think they're hell on wheels. One dead and two pretty bad,' the two-striper answered.

'Locals?' I asked.

'Yeah. They ought to know better. Gravel edges are murder at high speed. You turn your head away for a second and you're gone. Especially if you've been on the turps.'

I nodded, noticing that the younger constable still couldn't tear his eyes way from my Nikon and the 400-mm lens. 'Doing a spot of photography?' he asked at last.

'Hoping to,' I said with a wry grin.

'I'm a camera bug myself but I can't afford the kind of gear you've got.'

'Like to take a look?' I asked.

'I sure would,' he said, his face lighting up.

'I'll focus it on that crow down the road a bit,' I said. When I had the lens homed in on the big black bird I stepped aside.

'You travelling through or staying a while?' the two-striper asked me.

'I could be staying for a little while. You fancy a cuppa?' I asked.

'Thanks,' he said.

'Milk . . . sugar?'

'Both, thanks.'

I went and got extra cups out of the vehicle along with some teabags and sugar. 'Help yourself,' I said.

The younger man straightened and let out his breath. 'What a lens. My biggest is a 200 mm. Looks like I'll need to start saving for a 400 mm,' he said.

'Depends on what you want to do with a camera. You can take good pics without a 400 mm but if you want to do wildlife photography, especially birds, you'll need one eventually. But we've all got a lot to learn. You never know it all,' I said. 'Do you want a bit of tucker to go with that tea?'

He looked at his partner and then nodded. After making his tea I buttered a couple of slices of wholemeal bread, put it on a plate and held it out to them. Each man took a slice without hesitation. Looked like they mightn't have had a chance to have breakfast before they were called out to the accident.

When he'd finished eating, the two-striper looked at me and frowned thoughtfully. 'Do I know you?' he asked.

'I doubt it,' I said.

'You look familiar,' he persisted. 'I've seen your face somewhere.'

'Not on any wanted posters, I assure you,' I said with a laugh. 'How long have you been in the force?'

'Nearly ten years,' he said.

'Who's the ranking officer in Coona these days?' I asked.

'Senior Sergeant Morris,' the two-striper answered. 'You in the Force?'

'I used to be . . . CIB,' I said, wondering if it was the same Morris who'd received a gong for bravery during a flood. If so there was a good chance that he'd remember me because I received my gong at the same function. 'Will Senior Sergeant Morris be at the station today?'

The two-striper nodded. 'He sometimes goes home for lunch between one and two. But not every day. It depends what's on.'

'Could you tell him to expect a visitor,' I asked.

'Sure. What did you say your name was?' the older constable asked me.

'I didn't,' I said, smiling, not about to fall for that old trap. 'I have a very good reason for not wanting my name flashed about. Let's just leave it that I'm here with the Commissioner's blessing. But I don't want that flashed around either.' I reckoned that mentioning the PC would curtail any more questions.

The two men looked a bit nonplussed at this revelation and soon after got up, thanked me for the tea and turned to leave.

'You might care to do a spot of photography with me some time,' I said to the younger cop.

'I'd like that,' he said with a grin. 'How should I get in touch with you?'

'You'll be able to do that through Senior Sergeant Morris, Constable . . . ?'

'Beattie. Graham Beattie,' he said.

After their car had disappeared into the distance I began packing my gear. The two-striper had looked at the number-plates of my 4WD and then written something down, probably my car's rego details. They'd probably pass the 4WD's registration number on to Coonabarabran station. Both men seemed good types and were probably good police officers too.

After one last look around I packed away my photography gear, put the tea and food away and got out the big map of the area showing the location of all the properties with details of who owned them. Though it wasn't right up to date because some properties had probably changed hands, it provided a lot of essential information about roads and lesser tracks in the Pilliga.

After a thorough scrutiny of the map and with the belief that I had the overall picture of the Pilliga back in my head, I folded up the map and got in the vehicle.

CHAPTER 9

As soon as I hit Coonabarabran I headed straight for the cop shop. There were two marked police cars and some unmarked vehicles, mostly Holdens, in the car park at the station. After parking my vehicle I walked to the front of the building.

Inside, a different two-striper and a slightly smaller constable were at the front desk. They gave me the usual intense scrutiny characteristic of police officers. The good ones, anyway.

'Good morning,' I said brightly. 'Is Senior Sergeant Morris available?'

'Who shall I say wants to see him?' the big two-striper asked.

'Can you just tell him I'm the gent his boys had a cuppa with on the Binnaway Road after the accident this morning.'

I could tell by the looks on the faces of both men that my morning visitors had discussed me. The two-striper picked up a phone and spoke into it briefly. Hanging up, he asked me to follow him and we walked into the inner recesses of the station, where he stopped and knocked at the door of a closed office. After the occupant had called for me to come in he thanked the two-striper who nodded and closed the door again.

The officer at the desk got up as I entered, his expression one of surprise as he came over to shake my hand. 'I don't believe it. Lachie Sinclair, the fellow who nailed Bud Hollis and took a bullet doing it,' he said with a grin as we shook.

'Senior Sergeant Morris, the fellow who rescued a woman and her two kids from a car during a raging flood,' I countered.

'Not bad, Lachie,' Morris said. 'What the blazes are you doing here?'

'What I've come to talk to you about will take a while to tell, Senior Sergeant,' I said to Morris, who was a tall man but not bulky.

'Ming to you, Lachie,' he said.

We sat down and he got the young constable at the front desk to bring us tea and biscuits. While we waited I had a good look at him and saw he hadn't put on a lot of weight since I'd last seen him. He had a good head of greying hair and slightly olive skin. A wide red scar protruded some three or four inches beyond the neck of his blue shirt and I remembered he'd also been commended for rescuing a family from a fire. He clearly hadn't escaped unscathed. I'd say that there weren't many braver police officers than Morris.

After the tea and biscuits arrived he picked up one of his phones and growled into it. 'No more calls for me until further notice.'

Sipping his tea he regarded me with unconcealed interest. 'When the boys came back from that accident and mentioned meeting an ex-cop with a lot of fancy camera gear who wouldn't give them his name, I never imagined it would be you. Why isn't your vehicle registered in your name?' he asked.

'I didn't give your fellows my name because I don't want it splashed around the district.'

'So you're here on a case?' he asked.

I nodded and filled him in on how I'd set up in security and PI work since I'd left the force. Then I proceeded to detail the reason for my visit. He listened attentively, occasionally stopping me to ask a question.

'So you see Ming, it's more than likely that I'll need your help before this race is run. I can tell you that your Super at Mudgee will be briefed by Sydney and he'll be instructed to tell you I'm to be given any assistance I require. Sydney wanted your Super to brief you before I arrived but I asked them to leave it until I'd made contact with you. I'm not here to get in your way. And if those rotten bank robbers are here the only interest I'll have in them is whether they're holding Caroline Clemenger. I'm being paid by her mother,' I said.

'I see,' he said thoughtfully, clearly weighing up all I'd told him.

'Have you made any progress or come to any conclusions about Caroline Clemenger's whereabouts?' I asked.

'The answer to both your questions is no. But the truth of the matter is that my hands are tied. I was asked not to do anything until there was a ransom demand. There hasn't been one. I would have raided the Challis property but was instructed not to because the big chiefs in Sydney thought it might scare the bank robbers into running and possibly killing their hostage,' said Morris.

'Have you heard anything that might suggest they're hiding somewhere in the Pilliga?' I asked.

'No. Only that Head Office think Ted Challis was the third man in the bank robbery,' said Morris. 'Is that why you're here?'

'A couple of things we've heard suggest they may well be in the Coonabarabran region. And as you're aware, Sheila Cameron says she saw Caroline Clemenger sitting in a car in the main street here. Superintendent Ballinger didn't put much credence in that sighting because it seemed so strange that any crims would bring a hostage into town. But Sheila's a long-time family friend of mine and I'm going to see if I can get the full facts from her. However, the bottom line is that Sheila's a smart woman and went to the same school as Caroline Clemenger, so if she says she saw her I think there's a good chance she did,' I said.

'Okay, Lachie. Let's get down to tin tacks. How can I help you?' Morris asked.

Though I didn't show it I felt a huge sense of relief. Having Morris onside and willingly cooperating with me was going to make my job a lot easier. 'Nix, right at this moment. I may need little bits of information from time to time and I hope to be able to keep you informed too. As I said, if I locate these creeps, they're yours. My main brief is to locate and – if she's still alive – rescue Caroline Clemenger,' I said.

'Thanks Lachie,' said Morris, possibly thinking what the apprehension of the bank robbers might mean for his station. 'How long have you got?'

'As long as it takes,' I said.

'It could be risky, Lachie, one man out in the bush on his own. Shouldn't we provide you with someone as back-up?' asked Morris.

'The Sydney chiefs reckon I've got a far better chance of finding the bank robbers and working out if they're holding Caroline Clemenger if I'm on my own. I know it's highly irregular but this case calls for irregular handling. And I do have a contingency plan to fall back on if the going looks too much for one man,' I said.

Morris thought about what I'd said for a bit and then seemed to make up his mind. 'I wouldn't like to see you killed and dumped somewhere in the Pilliga, so keep in touch and don't hesitate to ask if you need help. Once you locate those mongrels we can deal with them,' he said.

'That's more or less what I'm planning to do. Superintendent Ballinger has already approved me calling on the services of my old partner in the force, DI Luke Stirling to help me. But I think it would look too suspicious having another bloke with me.'

'There'll be no need for you to import anyone,' Morris said mildly.

'That's great, Ming. I'm not here to embarrass you and if we play our cards right, maybe we'll both win big. I came here as my first port of call because I always try and do the right thing by the local police. Now what do you reckon?' I asked.

Morris held out his hand. 'We'll give you all the help you need,' he said.

'Thanks, Ming. I'll make sure you don't regret it.'

'I hope not. You going out to the old place?' he asked.

'I'll be going out to see my mother. I'd really appreciate it if you don't let on who I am for the time being. It'd be great to have some breathing space before the word gets out that I'm up here. If these crims are around and at all smart, they might just put two and two together,' I said.

'You're asking for the impossible, Lachie,' Morris protested. 'You're well known in this town and district. The first person who spots you will have it around the district inside a few hours.'

'I don't aim to be spotted. And maybe I'll only need a few days. Do you know much about the Challis family?' I asked.

'Billy Challis was seriously injured in that accident just down the road from where you were camped last night. He's been taken to Dubbo Hospital. His mate was killed.'

'How many of them are there?' I asked.

'Too many. Then again, one would be too many of that family. They're not much chop. There's old man Challis and then there's Ted and Peter and Jack and Billy. Peter is the pick of the boys. He's working on a property near Coonamble. There are two girls as well. One of them works in town and the other does odd jobs,' said Morris.

'Have you seen Ted lately?' I asked.

'No, he's the only member of the family we haven't seen. The Sydney boys told me he was living with a woman at Bondi a while ago but hasn't been seen for ages. I wouldn't think Ted was bright enough to organise a big bank robbery,' said Morris.

'Probably not. But he might have been bright enough to drive the getaway vehicle. Did Sydney mention anything of the kind to you?' I asked.

'They asked us not to go making enquiries about him, and just to keep a watching brief out for him and let them know if he surfaces. So far he hasn't,' said Morris.

'The police are hoping Ted will lead them to the other two blokes. If you haven't seen him he's probably lying low and the best place to do that is in the Pilliga. His known associates are all Sydney blokes. The big question is whether he and his crim mates are here or somewhere else. Though it's not as salubrious as the

Gold Coast, it's probably a lot safer for crims, and he hasn't been sighted anywhere else,' I said.

'Okay, Lachie,' said Morris.

'Where do the Challises hang out?' I asked.

'They've got a big old weatherboard house in town and a bit of land out near the Gorge. The old man and Rita live mainly in town though old Charlie goes out to the property fairly often. Charlie's dodgy but not big time. We're fairly certain he's been mixed up in stock stealing over the years but we've never been able to nail him. We've inspected cattle at his yards on the Gorge property and never found a trace of a stolen beast. His boys would know that area like the back of their hands. Beyond the Challis place it's all heavy timber and you'd need an army to search it. Cattle probably couldn't survive in there anyway. But Charlie and his neighbours have got some hundreds of acres of cleared country where cattle do all right. He's as cunning as a bush rat and he's been too clever for us,' Morris admitted.

'What's out at the Gorge these days?' I asked.

'It's a designated camping ground and one of the nicest spots in the Pilliga. There's a little creek with a small waterfall above a rock pool about the area of a fifty metre swimming pool. There are no amenities, though there's been talk of putting toilets and a shower unit there. There's a timber lease on the other side of the creek and just up the road you come to the first house. The Challis place adjoins it. There's koalas in the trees along the creek,' said Morris.

'The Gorge seems the right place to make a start then, so I'll give it the once-over first. If I come away with the slightest suspicion

Caroline Clemenger is being held out there, I might need to import a policewoman to help me out. A local might be recognised,' I said.

Morris looked at me aghast. 'That's a bit over the fence, Lachie. What's your idea?'

'I'm going to poke about posing as a wildlife photographer. I've got all the gear for it. It's a good enough cover but a woman would probably add more legitimacy.'

'I wouldn't feel comfortable asking a female officer to go bush with you, Lachie. You're not even a police officer now so asking for a policewoman to work with you would be very irregular. Anyway, where would she sleep and all that sort of thing?'

'I'd move into my vehicle and she could have my tent. She'd be working undercover. Only thing is that she'd have to take her directions from me.'

'If you were still in the Force it might be a different matter, but there's just no way I could sanction a civilian giving orders to a police officer,' said Morris.

'Well rather than calling them orders, we could call them suggestions she'd be well advised to accept. Anyway, as I said before everything I'm doing is irregular because it's an irregular sort of case,' I said calmly.

'But there's a fair degree of risk. I know you were a good detective and the Sydney brass are supporting you, but if anything goes wrong it'll be me who cops the flak,' he said.

'Not necessarily. If Ballinger sends me a female officer and anything goes wrong it'll be Sydney that cops the flak. But that's assuming the worst possible outcome. I'm trying to come at these fellows, if they're around here, in a way that doesn't involve gunplay,' I said.

'How did Ballinger react when you said you might want a female cop?' Morris asked.

'He doubted whether the Commissioner would agree but he didn't turn me down flat. He knows I wouldn't suggest anything unless I had a good reason,' I said.

'I'll think about it and maybe talk to Ballinger,' said Morris.

'That's okay. I may not need anyone at all. These guys may not even be here anyway,' I said.

'If you're going into the Pilliga to look for crims why don't you use a male officer as back-up? It's far too risky going out on your own but I'd prefer a bloke to a woman,' said Morris.

I shook my head. 'As I said to the Sydney brass, two men poking about just wouldn't look right.'

'I suppose you're armed?' he said.

I nodded.

'Can I see it?' he asked.

I took out my gun and passed it across to him.

'A Browning, eh,' he said, giving it a thorough inspection before he handed it back to me. 'How long has it been since you've last used a gun?' he asked.

'I keep up the practice,' I said. 'As for the Browning, I don't like running short of bullets. A six-shot was once nearly the death of me. I also have a Mannlicher rifle with scope sight and a double barrel twelve gauge.'

'I hope you don't have to use any of them while you're here,' he said.

'Me, too. But if I do it'll only be because I have to. The fellows who robbed the bank were both armed,' I said.

He nodded. Police took the view that any crim with a firearm was likely to use it.

After a bit more chat about local stuff Ming scribbled something on his pad and tore off the page and gave it to me. 'The top number is this station. The second one is my home number and the bottom one is my mobile number. Ring me at any hour if you need help,' he said.

'Thanks,' I said, taking the piece of paper. 'Now, if you're agreeable I'd like to route all messages to and from me via this station. Right now I'd like to send an email to Superintendent Ballinger.'

'Good idea. We'll send it on the way out. Let's have that bit of paper back and I'll add our email particulars.

I wrote out my message and handed the pad back to him. It read:

Have made contact with Senior Sergeant Morris/
Coonabarabran, who is extending full cooperation. Please use
this number for all messages directed to me. Please do not,
repeat not, use my name in messages. Use instead L. Rivers.

I have informed SS Morris that I may need a female police
officer to add legitimacy to my cover. Could you please
examine who is available in this field should I need her?

Morris looked at me in a funny kind of way. He'd probably never been involved with a private investigator who corresponded with the head brass in Sydney as if he was one of them.

Ballinger would probably bust his gut when he read my message and it was odds on that he'd get in touch with Morris quickly to try and find out what I actually knew. I thought there was a good chance that I'd get my policewoman. Just who I'd get was another matter.

'You're presuming a lot,' said Morris.

'I have a funny feeling about this case,' I said.

I stood beside Morris as he typed out my message wondering if I'd been a bit high-handed. It's true that what I was asking for was a bit irregular but if it produced results that would be all that mattered to the police. There was nothing they hated so much as an unsolved crime or a case that couldn't be closed because of insufficient evidence.

'Where can we get hold of you?' Morris asked.

'I'll be with my sister and her husband tonight. He's the accountant, Laurie Stratton. If you come looking for me please use an unmarked vehicle and no uniforms,' I told him.

'Is that where you're heading now?' he asked.

'That's right. My sister Flora and Sheila Cameron have been friends for years and I need to talk to Sheila about whether she's sure it was Caroline Clemenger she spotted in that car,' I said.

'You'll have a job remaining anonymous if anyone sees you with Sheila Cameron,' Morris said with a broad grin. 'You might as well use a loud hailer. I'll give it a day and the whole district will know. Give it a week and they'll have you engaged to Sheila.'

'They won't see me with her. We'll meet for dinner at Laurie and Flora's place,' I said.

'Did Sheila say anything about the people who were with Caroline Clemenger?' Morris asked.

'Mrs Kendall was vague about that. She mustn't have asked for descriptions of the men,' I said.

'It seems there's a lot I don't know about,' Morris said harshly.

'Well I'm telling you what I know and if I learn anything worthwhile from Sheila I'll pass it on pronto. I can understand why the Sydney boys are treading so lightly. If I locate the bank robbers and they or you move on them and Caroline Clemenger is killed – that's supposing she's still alive – there'll be a hell of a ruckus. Her mother wields a lot of influence,' I said.

I was halfway to the front door when Morris called me back and nodded towards the screen on his computer. Open on it was an email saying:

Perfectly content that Mr Rivers can handle the C matter.

Mr Rivers must have a very good reason re his enquiry about the availability of a Sydney policewoman. This matter has now been discussed and approved at the highest level. If the request is made I have just such an officer in mind and I think she would suit the role admirably. She would have to volunteer as I wouldn't order a female officer to go bush with Mr R. It is very irregular but Mr R produces results. We have a lot of faith in him.

R. Ballinger Supt

'It seems to me that you might just as well still be in the Force,' said Morris.

'I've got a lot more freedom of action now. I'm not tied down by regulations. I'd appreciate it you get back to Ballinger and thank him on my behalf.'

He nodded and I left the station and walked across the parking lot to my vehicle. I had hardly reached it when I was halted by a shout from Morris who was standing outside the front door of the station. 'Hang on, Lachie. Ballinger's already emailed back.'

I walked back to the station and looked at the return email, which had been marked urgent.

Two men wearing balaclavas and gloves held up a branch of the United Bank on the North Shore. Same MO as Sydney job, third man drove getaway vehicle. Teller shot and wounded. Preliminary estimate of haul is over $100,000.

If above men prove to be the ones you're looking for in your area, please advise Mr Rivers to approach with extreme caution.

R. Ballinger Supt

I handed the message back to Morris whose face had noticeably hardened. 'Does this increase or lessen your chances of getting a policewoman?' he asked.

'I think it'll depend on future developments,' I said.

'She'll need to know what she might be getting into,' said Morris.

'They'll lay all that on the line,' I said, preparing to leave again.

'Good luck, Lachie,' said Morris.

'I'll be talking to you. Thanks for your support in all this,' I said.

As I got in my car I felt a surge of relief. Morris was a straight shooter and I couldn't have had anyone better to back me up.

CHAPTER 10

My mind turned off Morris and Caroline Clemenger when I got in the car because the meeting I was going to organise with Sheila Cameron rammed home the fact that I still wanted a wife but I was also dead scared of making another mistake. Two failures would be too much to take. My ideal woman would be someone who'd been reared in the bush and preferably wanted to live on a property and have some kids. I reckoned I probably had only one more chance at a successful marriage and it was important that my next partner wanted more or less what I did.

Despite the issues we'd had with Father as kids I felt lucky to have been brought up on a farm with plenty of open spaces, close to the sources of food and with dogs, horses and decent air to breathe. The truth of the matter was that I'd never felt completely comfortable living in a city. I missed the community feeling of a country town and the closeness to nature. But I needed to put all thoughts of marriage and children away until I'd established whether Caroline Clemenger was dead or alive.

I put on my dark glasses and donned my wide-brimmed Akubra,

hoping they'd be sufficient to allow me to get to Flora's house without anyone recognising me. Bush people don't miss much. They see a strange vehicle, a strange new vehicle, and they take an immediate interest in its ownership. Unless a Rolls Royce or a Lamborghini was involved, most vehicles didn't rate a second look in the city. There were too many of them. But the appearance of a strange new four-wheel drive in Coonabarabran was another matter.

If the same three men had committed this latest bank heist, as suggested by the similarity of the MO, it could mean that Caroline Clemenger didn't need guarding anymore because she was dead. However, there was also the possibility that word had reached the crims that Ted Challis had been sighted in the first robbery, causing them to use a different driver and leaving Ted to keep an eye on Caroline Clemenger.

I snapped my mind back to family matters because I was getting close to Laurie and Flora's big bungalow and I needed Flora to get Sheila to her house so I could talk to her. I had no idea what Sheila thought of me now but she couldn't be told I was at Flora's in case she refused to come. I knew she was crooked on me for picking Fiona over her but she had never married so she might be crooked on all men.

After parking I walked around the small veggie garden to the back door. The kids would be at school and Laurie at work.

'Lachie,' Flora cried when she opened the door. 'Oh, it's so good to see you and you couldn't have come at a better time.

'Hey sis,' I said as she flung her arms round my neck.

'What brings you here, Lachie?' she asked after she released me. 'Can you stay for lunch?'

'Dinner, too, if you'll have me,' I said, smiling.

'Terrific,' she said leading me out to the kitchen with a huge smile on her face. 'What's doing? Lachie?' she asked.

'I'm here on a case but it'd be great if you could keep that quiet. How's your crew?' I asked, biting a stick of celery.

'Laurie's business is doing well but he's still putting in too many hours. And now some of his mates are trying to talk him into running for mayor. God knows when we'll see him if he does and he's elected. The kids are doing well. Brett topped his grade last year and Katrina is doing really well in English,' said Flora.

We chatted more about the kids and their friends. Flora and Laurie had decided not to send either Brett or Katrina away to school, which I completely understood.

'How's Sheila?' I asked after a while.

'She's in great form. She's enjoying her new receptionist role at the surgery that opened here recently. We had lunch the other day and she was asking about you,' said Flora.

'I really need to speak with her about the case I'm up here working on. Is there any chance you could invite her over after work? Best not to let her know I'm here until she arrives though,' I said.

'Sure,' said Flora. 'Is the case you're up here on about Caroline Clemenger's disappearance?'

'Yes,' I said, 'but I'll tell you more later.'

Flora finished preparing lunch and then went off to find the phone, complaining all the while about how the kids never put it back after they'd finished with it. After a while I heard her chatting and laughing and before long she was back saying, 'She'll be here about sixish. She just needs to finish updating a couple of files. I didn't tell her you were here. It might sound silly but I don't think Sheila has ever got over you opting for Fiona. Like me, she thought you were both making a mistake and we were right,' she said.

'That you were,' I said, 'but we have to look forward, not back, don't we? There wouldn't be a forty odd per cent divorce rate if we all made the right choices,' I said.

It was great to catch up with Flora and we'd been having a good yarn about everything and I was on my second cup of tea when she told me about Nicole and Stuart. 'Their marriage is as good as over, Lachie. Vickie's threatening to leave home too. After spending all that time studying at ag college she was keen to make some changes at Kamilaroi. Well, she wanted to take up showing sheep and cattle again but Stuart told her she couldn't. Now all she wants to do is get out. Nicole is furious with Stuart about it.

'A lot of the trouble is because Stuart wanted Nicole to have another child in the hope she'd have a boy. Nicole doesn't have any intention of getting pregnant though. Quite apart from anything she feels too old. The three girls have been drawn into their marriage problems because Stuart has been going off his brain about her refusal to try for another child. So there's Kamilaroi with no son and heir on the horizon and Stuart flatly refusing to allow Vickie any kind of a role on Kamilaroi,' she said and then broke off, looking like she was pondering on telling me other things.

'Is something else going on?' I asked.

'Well, yes, it seems as if Stuart has been seeing another woman,' said Flora.

'Christ, what an idiot,' I said, finding it hard to believe. 'He couldn't have a better wife than Nicole. In fact it beats me she's stuck with him for so long,' I said.

Flora agreed with me – she and Nicole had become good friends over the years and she understood how difficult things had been for her. After chatting about Nicole and Stuart a bit more, I told her how well my security firm had been going and how I'd become caught up in the search for Caroline Clemenger.

'I do wish you'd do something else, Lachie. You could have been killed when you were shot and now you're chasing more of the same. Mum worries about you all the time,' said Flora.

'It's what I know and what I was trained in, Flora. However, if it's any consolation to you I'm thinking of chucking it in. If I locate Caroline Clemenger and earn the reward her mother's offered, I'm thinking it'd be good to get myself some land,' I said.

'You don't have to keep doing something so dangerous anymore. Dad left you a third of Kamilaroi and you could come back, build a house and live there. You'd have a nice living with over ten thousand sheep and more than three hundred breeding cows. Mum would love you to come back here. We all would. It would be far better than gambling on a small farm with your limited resources,' said Flora.

'I'd still be too close to Stuart if I came back here. I'd have to use the Kamilaroi shearing shed or put up a separate shed. There'd be problems,' I said.

'There'll always be problems no matter what you do,' she said.

'Yeah, but there's some you can avoid and some you can't. Stuart is a problem I can still avoid. I've thought about cutting off a third of Kamilaroi and selling it but it took a long time for the family to put together that area of country and make all the improvements and I wouldn't like to be the one who presides over its dissolution. I'd feel lousy about that,' I said.

'Kind hearts don't pay the bills, Lachie. You're entitled to a third of Kamilaroi and you should utilise it,' said Flora.

'I've paid my own way ever since I left here and the only extra money I've had was my share of what Mum gave us all. I know Mum wants me to come back here but I don't want to come back and be fighting with Stuart. You know what he's like,' I said.

Flora agreed with that but still wasn't convinced that potential problems couldn't be avoided but before she could continue talking about it I changed the subject and we moved on to other things.

After lunch we washed up and then went back to the lounge where I filled Flora in more on the reason for my visit. 'You ever see her or anyone who resembles her?' I asked, showing her Caroline Clemenger's picture.

She shook her head. 'No, I haven't seen a woman remotely resembling her and I'd certainly remember if I had. She's really striking, isn't she? Not beautiful but a face you'd remember. Sheila was fairly certain it was her.'

'Yeah, that's the reason I need to speak to her. Between you and me we have some reason to believe that Caroline Clemenger is being held somewhere in the Pilliga. The evidence is sketchy but it's more than we've got for anywhere else,' I said.

'And you're being paid a lot of money to find her?' said Flora.

'That's right but I'm not anxious to have my presence here trumpeted around the district. I know how news spreads in these small country towns and I don't want the local rag advertising the fact that I'm here. If the men holding Caroline Clemenger read about an ex-cop and security guy coming up here they might put two and two together and come up with five,' I said.

'After you see Mum and hear about all the problems out there you may not feel like working. And you'll need to drill Brett and Katrina that although you're actually here, you're not here. I've got to go out now and pick up some more supplies for dinner. The kids will probably beat me home. Meanwhile, put the kettle on when you want a cuppa. There's fruit cake in the big red tin on the first shelf in the kitchen,' she said.

The house was very quiet after Flora left, which suited me down to the ground because I wanted to scour through some of the past editions of the local newspaper. It was usually full of town and district news, local sporting results and livestock prices, with an occasional snippet of juicy gossip. Nothing had changed there. I'd read through several of the most recent editions and was just about to give up when a small article caught my eye. It was to the effect that two local men, James Brewster and Zane Reid, had made a 'killing' at Randwick races. It seemed they'd put what they'd won on an outsider and won a heap of money.

Now that is interesting, I thought as I put down the paper. Why would two punters want to let everyone know they'd won a lot of money on the race track? Either they were flamboyant gamblers who liked to flaunt their success or men trying to mask sudden affluence under the guise of gambling. If either of those men was seen driving a flash new vehicle, the average person would attribute their sudden prosperity to their success on the racetrack. It seemed to me that advertising such success would be the kind of thing only a half-way smart crim would do.

I rang my Sydney office and when Christine answered I gave her Brewster and Reids' names and asked her to get Dasher working on them pronto. I told her I would phone her next day for the results.

I'd just put the phone down when I heard the kids' voices outside and next thing Brett and Katrina had let themselves in. They pulled up dead when they saw me.

'Hi guys,' I said, grinning at the mixed surprise and delight on their face.

'Uncle Lachie!' they shouted in unison and fell on me. They literally did. They were my favourite pair of kids, though Luke's kids ran them a close second. I always gave them a great time when they came to Sydney.

'What are you doing here, Uncle Lachie?' Brett asked when he finally stopped rumbling me.

'It's a long story, Brett. Very hush hush. You aren't to tell anybody that I'm here. Not a soul, you understand,' I said in my most serious voice.

Brett and Katrina both looked instantly serious. 'Is it an undercover job?' Brett asked. He was a great reader and had a vivid imagination.

'It would be if I was still in the police force. As it is, it's very serious detective work. Hey, Mum said something about a fruit cake. She's gone down town to buy a few things but she should be back pretty soon,' I said.

'I'll get it,' Katrina said and ran off to the kitchen.

'I must say you two have grown a heap since I saw you last,' I said as we all hoed into a piece of fruitcake each.

'So what's the *big* news in your life, Katrina?' I asked.

'There's no really big news, Uncle Lachie. I go out to Nanna's and do a bit of riding when Vickie and Shelley are on holidays. I also do a fair bit of swimming and I'm in the school team,' she said.

'Does Sergeant Morris coach you?' I asked.

'Yep. And he's really good. Tells lots of funny jokes too,' she said.

'What about you, Brett?' I asked.

'I'm in the first eleven at school and I've been getting some fair scores. I'm nowhere near as good as you were but the sports master says I'm good for my age. I play league in the winter. Dad says my marks are good enough for me to do medicine,' said Brett.

'That's great news,' I said. 'Maybe next time I come up we can have a few sessions in the nets.'

That'd be fantastic, Uncle Lachie,' said Brett.

I was well into my second slice of fruit cake when Flora returned.

'You look very smug,' she told me.

'Some things I may be but I refute smug. It's the feeling generated by my enjoyment of this scrumptious cake. I haven't tasted fruit cake like it for years. The bikkies aren't bad either,' I said.

'Hmm. Kids pleased to see you?' she asked.

'I think you could say that. Were you able to get the goodies?'

'Of course. I got a few other things too. It isn't every day you honour us with your presence, brother dear,' she said.

'Thanks, Flora.'

We spent the next couple of hours catching up with more local gossip, peeling green beans and spuds. After Brett and Katrina had finished their homework they dragged me away from the kitchen and into their respective bedrooms where they showed me photos of their various sporting triumphs and passed on their own version of local activities. I learned from Brett that Stuart had bought another racehorse which had cost a lot of money. This had led to a very big row between Stuart and Nicole. It seemed that Vickie had asked for a camera and Stuart had knocked her back. Nicole had told him that he could afford a racehorse so he should be able to shell out for a camera for his daughter, given her interest in becoming a photographer down the track. Stuart had responded by telling her that there was no way photography was going to feature in Vickie's future.

From Katrina I learned that Sheila didn't have a steady 'boyfriend'. Actually, she didn't have a boyfriend at all. And wasn't this a shame as she was so lovely. One choice titbit Katrina told me was that Vickie kept a picture of me and some cuttings about me being shot in a scrapbook in a drawer of her dressing table. According to Katrina she regarded me as some kind of hero. I thought this might be because she and her father didn't get on, and since I didn't get on with her father either it made me an ally.

'I'm not supposed to know but Uncle Stuart is supposed to have a secret lady friend,' Katrina said in a hushed voice, after making sure there was no-one outside the room. 'I heard Mum and Dad talking about it. The woman lives at Gunnedah and breeds horses. Uncle Stuart visits her. Isn't that awful? No wonder Auntie Nicole is going to leave him.'

I changed the subject, asking her how her horse riding was going. It was relaxing to be able to lie across the kids' beds while they talked about the things they enjoyed doing and their friends as well as passing on their 'secrets'. I'd love to have kids like these I thought as I lay there. A lot of water had flowed under the bridge since I left Kamilaroi and whatever else I had, I didn't have kids.

I was brought back to earth when I watched the early TV news and heard more details of the North Shore bank robbery, which provided a stark reminder of why I was in Coonabarabran. As the minutes ticked by I started to feel a shade apprehensive about meeting Sheila Cameron. It wasn't just meeting Sheila that concerned me but also what she could tell me about her apparent sighting of Caroline Clemenger because her account of things was likely to provide a crucial piece of evidence.

CHAPTER 11

When the front doorbell rang soon after the news was over Flora went to answer the door and I stood up and walked out to the kitchen. I would wait there while Laurie gave Sheila a sherry . . . or two. I spoke in low tones with Brett and Katrina who had both been briefed by their mother on the Fiona-Sheila-Lachie triangle. Katrina thought that I had made a 'tragic' mistake. If the past couple of hours were anything to go by, 'tragic' was a word Katrina used quite a lot now.

After fidgeting for a while, unable to be distracted by the kids any longer I decided it was time to front Sheila. As I walked into the lounge room, there she was sitting in one of the big lounge chairs beside the fireplace with a glass in her hand. No doubt about it, she was still lovely.

I shall never forget the look on Sheila's face when she saw me. Her face underwent so many changes it was difficult for me to gauge her true feelings. There was shock initially because I was probably the last person she expected to see that night. It took her a little while to recover her equilibrium and by the time she did

Laurie and Flora had quietly left the room.

Seeing Sheila again took me back to when she and I were both teenagers and just beginning to meet life front-on. It was strange that Sheila had never married, and if what Katrina had said was true she didn't even have a 'boyfriend', because she was a truly lovely, smart woman.

'This is a surprise. I had no idea you were back,' Sheila said after a while.

'Officially, I'm not. How are you, Sheila?' I asked.

'I'm well, Lachie. Was it your idea to invite me here tonight?' she asked.

'Yes, it was. I need to talk to you about a case I'm working on,' I said.

'Are you looking for Caroline Clemenger?' she asked.

'As a matter of fact, I am,' I said. 'I've been told you think you saw her.'

'I definitely did. I recognised her immediately. But Caroline didn't acknowledge me and perhaps she didn't recognise me. It's been a while since we were both at school,' she said.

'Can you tell me how you came to see her? Take your time and give me as many details as you can possibly remember,' I said.

'That's easy, Lachie. And there were a couple of things I didn't tell the detective who first showed me Caroline's picture because I wasn't sure if I should. I didn't want to make a big fuss in case it transpired that I'd made a mistake. You see I wasn't even aware that Caroline was still missing. I don't usually read the Sydney newspapers and since I got my new job at the clinic I rarely even have time to read the local paper. There might have been a fuss at the time she was abducted but I was overseas at that time and I didn't hear a thing,' she explained.

'So how did you come to see her?' I asked again.

'A man who wasn't a local came to the surgery one day just as we were closing. He'd cut his leg badly and it needed stitching. After Dr Watts stitched it, he gave the man a tetanus shot because the cut had been caused by an axe. He also gave him a prescription for antibiotics and told him to come back in ten days and he'd check to see if the wound had healed well enough to take the stitches out. I was locking up after him when I saw Caroline sitting in the back seat of a car. It was a cream Holden. The thing that surprised me was that I knew how wealthy Caroline's family are, yet the man alongside her was rough-looking with tatts and she was wearing an ugly shabby old grey dress. Something about that and the way she looked away sharply, as if she knew I'd recognised her, stopped me from greeting her. But by the time I'd finished locking up the surgery the car was gone,' she said.

'Can you describe the man with the cut leg?' I asked.

'A couple of things about him didn't gel. One is that he said he didn't have his Medicare card and paid in cash and the other was that he told me his name was Brian Challis. When I asked him if he was related to any of the local Challises, he looked guilty. "Distantly, and just visiting briefly," he said. He certainly didn't look like any of the local lot. He was a solid fellow with a kind of olive skin and dark brown hair and they're all just the opposite,' she said.

'Why do you think he used the name Challis? Wouldn't he have been wiser to use a name like Smith or Jones?'

'I've wondered about that since. I guess it meant he didn't have to risk making up an address I might know so he just gave me the town address of the Challis family which I would know,' said Sheila.

'Ah, that's interesting. You're probably right. Did he come back to get his stitches taken out?' I asked.

'No, we never saw him again,' she said.

'I don't suppose you happened to take a note of the registration number of the car, even part of the number?'

'No, I was totally focused on Caroline,' said Sheila.

'Are you sure it was Caroline?' I asked.

'Absolutely sure. As I said, that's why the old grey dress and the bloke she was sitting with surprised me,' she said.

'If the woman you saw was Caroline Clemenger – and I'm sure you're right – the fact that you didn't say hello to her may well have saved her life, Sheila. You've been a big help,' I said.

'Have I really?' she asked.

'Much more than you probably realise,' I assured her.

'What's this all about, Lachie?' she asked.

I told her about Mrs Kendall coming to see me and how I'd agreed to try to locate her abducted daughter, who might or might not be somewhere in this area,' I said.

'What's your next move?' she asked.

'Kamilaroi in the morning to see Mum and then back to business,' I told her.

'Please be careful, Lachie. I nearly died when I heard you'd been shot and were in hospital. I want Caroline to be rescued but can't you allow the police to do it?' she said.

'It's a tricky job, Sheila. Circumstances will dictate just how she can be rescued. That's if she's still alive to be rescued. But if the police go charging in after these crims she could be killed. There's also the fact she could testify against her abductors about the bank robbery, which means they may want to get her out of the way permanently,' I said.

Sheila looked so grim at that I decided to ask her if she'd like another sherry.

'I would, thank you,' she replied. 'You've bowled me over.'

'Sorry, Sheila. I've probably worried you enough for one day. Maybe we should see what Flora's cooked up for dinner.'

'Of course,' she said, looking around. 'How diplomatic of Laurie and Flora to leave us.'

'Flora tells me you're doing an Arts course externally,' I said.

'I don't want to be a doctor's receptionist forever, just as I didn't want to be a nurse forever,' she said. 'I fell into the receptionist's job because of my nursing certificates and because, well . . . Ah, here's Flora.'

'Are you two ready for dinner?' asked Flora.

'Are you sure you want me here for dinner too, Flora?' asked Sheila.

'Of course. You know very well that our invitations always include dinner,' said Flora.

Sheila looked sideways at me. 'Surely you want Lachie to your-selves the first night. Won't I be in the road?' she asked.

'You'd never be in the road, Sheila,' said Flora, giving her a hug. 'We insist you stay for dinner.'

'Then of course I'd love to have dinner with you,' said Sheila. 'I'd have brought some wine if I knew I'd be staying.'

'No need,' I said, retrieving a bottle of wine from the kitchen.

Sheila gave me a dazzling smile when she saw I'd left some flowers and chocolates at her place at the dinner table. I was very relieved because not only was I pleased to see her again but to be on pleasant terms with her. I could see that she was slightly on edge but her naturally sweet disposition and her evident closeness to Flora and Laurie kept her with us for a couple of hours.

After catching up with the latest news with Laurie and hearing all about what Sheila had been up to, I decided it was time to bring the evening to a close. Tomorrow would be a busy day and I needed to make a couple of phone calls.

'It's been good to see you again, Sheila,' I said as I walked her to her car. 'I meant what I said, Sheila. It's been great to meet up with you again. You're very much the same as I remember you.'

'But older and wiser, Lachie, and some of my illusions have been well and truly shattered,' she said.

'Mine too, Sheila. One thing I've learned is the futility of looking back. One must go on. I doubt there's a person in the world who hasn't made a mistake,' I said.

'I never really got over you, Lachie,' she said quietly.

'I'm sorry for that, Sheila. I made the wrong decision and I paid for it. I realise I hurt you in the process. That was never my intention. I'd like us to be friends. However, it's up to you, Sheila,' I said.

She turned to me before she got in her car. 'I've always been your friend, Lachie. Thank you for the flowers and the chocolates,' she said before giving me a quick kiss on my cheek and getting into her car.

I shook my head as she drove away, more certain than ever that I would never understand women.

Back inside, I rang Ming and apologised for the late call before saying, 'I need to see you first thing in the morning, Ming.'

'Developments?' he asked tightly.

'I think so. What time will you be at the station?' I asked.

'Would eighty-thirty be early enough for you?'

'That's fine. I'll be there spot on eight-thirty,' I said. 'Good night, Ming.'

I had a shower and then got into bed. It had been quite a day and reasonably productive all in all. In fact I couldn't believe how far I'd progressed. I was strongly of the opinion that James Brewster and Zane Reid were implicated in Caroline Clemenger's abduction and that they, with Ted Challis, were very probably the three men who had pulled the first Sydney bank job. Brewster and Reid may well have been involved in the North Shore job too.

However, as had been drilled into me in my early years with the police, suspicion was not proof. But it was the prerequisite to proof which was the situation that now confronted me. My first priority was to locate Caroline Clemenger and if possible, rescue her. My second priority was to identify the men who had abducted her. As I lay there going over every detail of the case in my mind, the most puzzling aspect was why the men holding her had brought her to town. It seemed to me to be a terrible error of judgement and perhaps signified that the leader of the outfit wasn't the half-smart crim I'd figured him to be. He'd have to be very arrogant and contemptuous of the police to imagine he could get away with that kind of behaviour.

Why would he do it? Was I missing something? I wondered. And then something clicked in my brain and various ideas began to come together. The top man was a half-smart fellow who was also a gambler. He wasn't the type of man who'd be happy to act as the custodian of a woman. That would be too onerous a task for a flash fellow like him. No, he'd hand her over to his lesser associates and let them do the minding. The Challis crew would be responsible for Caroline Clemenger, leaving the big shots free to rob banks and punt on horses. So how come the big shots, and I presumed they were the big shots, despite the false name given to Sheila at the surgery, risked coming out in the open with Caroline Clemenger?

I thought about that for a long time before an idea came to me from something Ming Morris had said that morning. He'd told me the police had been after the Challis crew for a while on suspicion of stock stealing but they'd never been able to catch them with any stolen cattle. Perhaps there'd been a time or two when the Challis clan had to turn Caroline Clemenger over to the boss man so they could go away and pinch stock. They probably lived on the sales of stolen cattle. It was just possible that the boss man had been looking after Caroline Clemenger when he cut his leg with the axe. So maybe the reason he'd had her in the car when he went to the surgery was because he couldn't risk leaving her when he was forced to go to Coonabarabran to get his leg stitched. He, or they, would probably have had to take her.

The possibility that this was the solution made sense because surely only necessity would have compelled the crims to take Caroline Clemenger with them to Coonabarabran. Maybe the top man hadn't trusted his immediate offsider enough to leave Caroline in his care. Maybe, if he was a 'hard' man he would have got rid of her and the fact that he hadn't meant she was still alive. It was all theorising but until I had some hard evidence theorising was all I could do.

My thoughts turned briefly from Caroline Clemenger to Sheila Cameron and then, reluctantly, to Fiona. I wondered if I would ever again meet a woman capable of making my heart race like it had with Fiona. I hadn't found myself experiencing any sudden rush for Sheila. Not that she wasn't lovely and I had no doubt that she would make a good wife and mother. But she wasn't interested in life on a property and although she'd probably endure it for the right man, her heart would never be in it. Also, I yearned for a woman whose presence hit me like a tonne of bricks. Fiona had hit me like that when she gave herself to me but our marriage hadn't lasted because our priorities had been so different. If I'd learned anything from my failed marriage it was that, ideally, the woman you married should share some of your priorities. That was the ideal formula for a successful marriage. Ah, but I was day-dreaming. Or night dreaming. Very soon I slept.

CHAPTER 12

Ming Morris seemed a great deal more relaxed at our second meeting. He'd been affable enough the day before, though I think he'd felt a bit overwhelmed initially. He probably hadn't known how to take me and although he'd agreed to cooperate he hadn't really got right on side until after the exchange of emails and faxes between Superintendent Ballinger and me. I couldn't blame him for his initial diffidence because his natural instinct would be that the police were the best people to handle crime and criminals.

The police were always grateful for any help the public might give them, but when it came to the possibility of the public acting in the capacity of police, that was a different matter. If I'd been a run-of-the-mill private investigator rather than a former detective, and a decorated detective into the bargain, and if I'd turned up without official backing, Morris would have shown me the door. Despite his apparent willingness to cooperate, I could tell Morris wasn't entirely comfortable about me freelancing in the Pilliga. I didn't hold it against him. Morris was a good conscientious cop who didn't relish the thought of me being killed by criminals on his watch.

'I've been talking with Dick Ballinger,' he said by way of greeting. 'They're under very heavy pressure about these bank jobs. The banks are very jittery. There's a lot of money gone west – much more than the media has reported and he's very keen for me to cooperate with you as much as possible.'

I took that in and thought about it. Ballinger clearly realised I was a good bet and had decided to back me to the hilt. He knew I'd been offered a big financial inducement to locate Caroline Clemenger and that if I was able to find her I would also find the men who'd pulled the first Sydney bank job and most probably the second robbery given the similarity of the MO. Ballinger knew from experience that I wouldn't give up and I was probably his best chance of closing out the case because of my local knowledge.

'All being well, there won't be any more bank robberies. Not by the same men, anyway. I think I know who they are,' I said.

Morris looked at me in amazement. 'What have you got, Lachie?' he asked.

'Before I go into what I'm thinking I need some additional information. I had two lucky breaks yesterday. Can you show me where old man Challis has his place?'

'Sure,' said Morris before getting up and walking over to a big map on his office wall and pointing to an area I knew about but had never visited. 'That's the Challis place,' he said.

'Okay, and do you know where a character by the name of James Brewster lives?' I asked. 'It's not in town because I looked him up in the phone book.'

'I don't know but Ray Milson probably will. He comes from here and knows everybody,' said Morris.

'Would you mind getting him in here because I'd like to ask him a few questions?' I said.

Morris picked up his phone and presently the big senior constable who'd been on the desk the previous day came through the door.

My mobile phone rang at that precise moment. It was Dasher Doyle telling me that James Brewster had incurred a minor speeding fine but there was nothing listed against anyone by the name of Zane Reid.'

'Very interesting. Thanks a lot, Dasher,' I said, before ringing off and looking over at the two big men opposite me.

'Sit down, Ray,' said Morris. 'For the benefit of our discussion this is Mr Rivers. He has a few questions for you. He's on our side so you can be perfectly frank with him.'

Milson nodded. 'I've got a very good idea who he is but if you say he's Mr Rivers, that's who he is.'

'Do you know a guy called James Brewster?' I asked.

'Yeah, he owns a place out near the Gorge,' said Milson. 'And he spends a lot of time with the Challis boys who have the adjoining farm.'

'What can you tell me about Brewster?' I asked.

'His old man, Joe Brewster, left his farm to him. Old Joe was a real bushman. He could split posts, shear sheep, divine water, break in a horse and fight like a thrashing machine. Kick, bite, bollock and fetch your own doctor. That was Joe Brewster. He married a town woman and they only ended up having James before the wife cleared out and left him to rear the boy. Apparently she couldn't take living in the Pilliga.

'I think old Joe must have been pretty hard on James because as soon as he was old enough he cleared out to Sydney. He was a pretty flashy kid and a big talker and I've heard around the traps that he said there was no way he wanted to earn a living the way his old man had. No splitting posts for him. He had big ideas about making a lot of money. He was a bit wild and he got into trouble of some sort but he finished an apprenticeship,' said Milson.

'What trade was it?' I asked.

'Watchmaking. Apparently he'd always been very good with his hands,' said Milson. 'Last time I spoke to old Joe before he died he told me James was managing some jewellery place in Yankee Land.'

'A jewellery place?' I said, thinking who better to understand the value of Caroline Clemenger's jewellery than a man who'd managed a jewellery store. Various things were all starting to fall into place.

'Yeah, Old Joe said he was doing okay,' said Milson.

'So what brought James back to the Pilliga Scrub?' I asked.

'Joe died and left him the place. It's a pretty ordinary place, though it's mostly cleared and capable of running livestock. Apparently Brewster came back to sell the property but he's still around,' said Milson.

'Has he got any sort of a record in Australia?' I asked.

'We picked him up for speeding a few months ago. Like I said, there were a couple of minor offences before he left Australia,' said Milson.

'Do you recall what he was driving?' I asked.

'It was a cream Holden, though you'd hardly have known because it was so covered in mud and dust. The last time I saw him he was driving a flashy blue Mazda though,' said Milson.

'So what are you thinking, Lachie?' asked Morris.

'I'm beginning to suspect James Brewster and a bloke calling himself Zane Reid are implicated in Caroline Clemenger's abduction. And I also think they and Ted Challis might have pulled off the first Sydney bank job. They probably did the second heist too but that remains to be seen,' I said.

The two cops stared at me intently.

'You've made some awfully fast deductions since you left me yesterday, Lachie,' he said sternly.

'Well it's only a hypothesis at the moment but let me tell you what I think . . .' I said.

'First, Caroline Clemenger was wearing very expensive jewellery the day she was abducted. I think there's a chance she either lost her memory when her head hit the front door of the bank or, possibly, she's feigning loss of memory. They probably took her hostage because one of the crims knew enough about jewellery to realise she had plenty of money. Now we discover that James Brewster was a watchmaker and had managed a jewellery store,' I said, pausing briefly to let it sink in.

'According to Sheila Cameron a man came into the doctors' surgery she works at to get his leg stitched. Afterwards she saw him get into a cream-coloured car – the same car she'd glimpsed Caroline Clemenger sitting in the back seat of. I've been wracking my brains to work out why the crims would risk bringing Caroline into Coonabarabran and I think you might have given me the answer yesterday,' I said, looking at Morris. 'They must have had to bring her with them because they were looking after her at the time.

'You might well ask why they'd tie themselves down looking after a woman and not get other people to and I've been wondering about that too,' I said. 'Then yesterday you told me you'd been after old man Challis for stock stealing And I suspect that's what they were doing when Brewster cut his leg with the axe. They'd have been looking after Caroline Clemenger while the Challis crew were away. So you see they'd have been forced to take Caroline with them,' I said.

'Did Brewster give his name to Sheila Cameron?' asked Morris.

'No, he didn't. The appointment was made in the name of Brian Challis. But Sheila knows the family and she says there is no such person,' I said. 'Why he'd use that name is beyond me at this stage. He could have used any name at all. But he did give his address as the Challis address here in town.'

Morris still looked a bit incredulous so I handed him the newspaper clipping featuring Brewster and Reid. After he'd scanned it he handed it to Milson who read it and passed it back to me.

'I read that story,' said Morris.

'Make anything of it?' I asked.

'No, nothing beyond the fact that those two characters won a heap of money at Randwick races. That's the kind of small town gossip the local paper thrives on. I did vaguely wonder why anyone would be interested in passing on the story. Most people who win a lot of money aren't anxious to advertise the fact. There's an odd smart arse who likes to trumpet his or her cleverness but not many,' said Morris.

Milson nodded his agreement.

'You're dead right,' I agreed. 'Most gamblers try and conceal what they've won for a variety of reasons. I think Brewster deliberately sought out publicity through a newspaper to account for his sudden affluence. That way, when people see him driving around in a flash car, the first thing they think is he bought it from those winnings they read about or heard about on the race track. Some of it might have – because he'd need to have been sighted winning some punts – but a lot of it will have come from bank robberies. If I'm right – and I'm not claiming I am – Brewster made a couple of big mistakes.'

'You could be right, Lachie,' said Morris. 'It stands to reason that a fellow with a small property out in the Pilliga Scrub wouldn't make enough money to buy a flash car. But a couple of big wins on the race track could explain it. What do you think, Ray?' Morris asked his big offsider.

'Sounds plausible to me. And it's in keeping with Brewster to big-note himself too. As for the Challis lot, I wouldn't put anything past them. They're all as cunning as shithouse rats. Only Peter's any good and he doesn't have anything to do with the others,' said Milson.

'What can you tell me about Zane Reid?' I asked. 'If that's his name.'

'I've seen a Yank with Brewster at the pub a few times. Not sure of his name though. Tough looking fellow,' said Milson.

'The bloke who's holding the fort for me in Sydney while I'm up here told me he can't find any reference to a Zane Reid coming to Australia,' I said. 'Of course he could be using a false name.'

'Might have to get immigration involved,' said Morris.

'How long has Brewster been back in Australia?' I asked.

'Two years or thereabouts,' said Milson.

'Do you think there's enough in what I've said for me to call Ballinger with all this?' I asked Ming. Though I didn't really need to consult him, I thought he was a good cop and that it might help keep him on side.

'It's worth going through what you just told us. It's definitely feasible that Brewster, Ted Challis and this Zane character are the men we should be looking for. If any of the Challises are holding Caroline Clemenger they'll be complicit too,' said Morris.

'I think they *are* the men,' I said. 'I'll give him a call and see what he thinks.'

Sophie Walters answered. I knew her from my time in the force. She was some kind of assistant to Ballinger these days.

'Sophie, I need to talk to the Super. Can you please tell him that Lachie Sinclair wants to talk to him and that it's urgent.'

Ballinger was soon on the phone and he listened carefully to what I told him and agreed to seek information from immigration about the arrival into Australia of an American going by the name of Zane Reid. After we'd talked a bit more I told him it'd be a big help if he could send me up a female officer with weaponry experience as soon as possible because I intended going out to the Gorge to start staking out the Challises and Brewster. He said he'd get back to me.

Morris expressed surprise at the cooperation I was receiving from head office when I got off the phone. 'Do you do this sort of thing very often, Lachie?' he asked. 'I mean, ask to borrow female police officers for your cases?'

'I've never had to do so before,' I admitted. 'But Ballinger knows the police will get the credit for anything I achieve.'

Ming and I discussed a few more aspects of the case and I wound things up, keen to head off and start planning things. As we parted Ming said, 'Ballinger said you were as good as they come. I'm beginning to see why.'

'Thanks,' I said. 'If you can't inspire trust and faith with the people you work with, the game's not worth playing. Look what happened in Queensland with rotten apples at the top. And New South Wales has had its share of problems too. If we nail this mob I hope you and your team come out of it really well.' And I meant every word. Police cop a lot of criticism at times but all in all they do a great job.

'Thank you for all the hard work you've been doing,' he said. 'Where are you heading now?'

'I'm going out to Kamilaroi to see Mum,' I said, thinking it'd be best to wait until I heard about the possibility of a female officer before rushing out to the Gorge. When I arrived there my first preference would be to appear as a genuine wildlife photographer out camping with my girlfriend.

I left Coonabarabran Police Station hoping I had enough information to help me locate and hopefully rescue Caroline Clemenger. Despite some mis-steps Brewster and Reid had to be reasonably smart or they'd have been picked up before now. They hadn't left fingerprints anywhere so the police couldn't identify them. Then again, all crims make mistakes and Brewster and Co had made a couple of boomers.

Still, it wasn't an open and shut case. If the police raided Brewster's property prematurely and it turned out to be clean they'd have egg on their faces. And if Caroline Clemenger was being held elsewhere, any police action could precipitate her death.

Yes, Caroline Clemenger would have to be winkled out of the crims' hands after careful investigation.

CHAPTER 13

Putting the Clemenger case out of my mind for the moment, I drove out towards Kamilaroi. I couldn't wait to see Mum, who still lived in the big Kamilaroi homestead we'd grown up in. These days she spent a lot of her time either gardening or painting landscapes.

I had to admit as I drove up the driveway to Kamilaroi that everything on the old place looked in great order. Much as I didn't like Stuart, it was clear that, like Father, he was a very competent property manager. The big hayshed was packed to the roof with bales of lucerne hay and all the grain silos – there were a dozen of them in a row – were no doubt full of feed oats and corn. The machinery was all under cover and there were no weeds growing about the sheds.

Kamilaroi had always been noted for both its sheep and cattle. Looking at the sheep near the driveway, they were as even as peas in a pod and had clearly been crutched fairly recently. The property's Hereford cattle had won numerous on-the-hoof awards and I noticed that many of the cows and younger cattle had red-brown markings around their eyes rather than the pure white head of old. Eye cancer was a perennial problem with white-faced Herefords so Stuart must have bought a couple of pricey bulls to breed more colour into them. He was a good manager, right enough.

I pulled up in the gravel drive and walked up the wide stone-flagged pathway to the front steps. It gave me a queer feeling to see the old homestead again. It felt so familiar. The long front veran-dah was almost exactly as I remembered it, with plenty of big easy chairs and pot plants. I felt a terrible pang when I walked past the window of Kenneth's room. I'd never get over his death as long as I lived.

Music was coming from inside the house so I rang the bell quite vigorously. The look of joy on Mum's face when she answered the door was wonderful to see.

'Lachie,' she cried. 'What are you doing here?'

'Coming to see you,' I said, taking her in my arms with a lump in my throat. 'How are you, Mum?'

'A lot better for seeing you,' she said.

I felt warmed by her words as well as regretful and guilty that I hadn't been up here since my father's funeral.

After exchanging kisses I followed Mum through to the kitchen where the kettle was in its usual place on the big Aga stove. A Cho-pin etude was coming from a CD player on the kitchen table and Mum leaned across and turned it off.

'What good timing,' she said. 'You're just in time for smoko. Oh, dear I don't have anything freshly made apart from a few old Anzac biscuits. If I'd known you were coming I'd have made short-bread,' she said.

'Anzacs will be wonderful, Mum. I've come to see you, not sample your larder,' I said.

'Since when have you not wanted to eat?' she said, smiling. 'I'll run you up some shortbread in no time at all.'

'That's great,' I said, happily. 'How are you really, Mum?'

'I'm as good as gold, Lachie. Physically, I've never felt better. I won first prize in the Coonabarabran art competition recently,' she said proudly.

'Yeah, Flora told me your painting was going great guns.'

'You've seen Flora? Why didn't she ring and tell me?'

'I wanted to surprise you. Also, I'm up here on sensitive work involving some local people and if word gets round that I'm in the district it might compromise things. In fact I wouldn't mind running my car into the garage alongside yours to avoid anyone seeing it.' I said. 'Are you expecting any visitors?'

'Either Stuart or Nicole call in every other day and sometimes one or the other has lunch with me. Nicole comes when Stuart is going to be away all day. How long are you staying?'

'I can only stay the day and night with you for the moment, but I'm hoping if I can close out this case reasonably quickly I'll be able to stay for a bit longer,' I said. 'I'm sorry I haven't been back for a while, Mum. I'm always so busy and I'm virtually a one-man show. I've got a secretary who helps out part time and an ex-cop who sometimes helps with overflow work but it's still hard to get a break.'

'Oh, Lachie, I do wish you would get out of security work and come back home to where you belong,' she sighed.

'I'd never entertain coming back while Stuart is here. You know that. I'm too used to running my own show,' I said.

'But you could build a house somewhere else on the place,' she said.

'How are the kids? And Nicole?' I asked, changing the subject.

'Don't let them hear you call them "kids". Vickie finished ag college last year. She worked so hard and I was so proud of her. But she and Stuart seem to have been arguing almost nonstop since the day she came back. Shelley's great and Maureen started at boarding school this year,' she said.

'That's no good about Vickie and Stuart,' I said. 'Poor kid. You should come down and stay with me for a while, I've got the house in good shape,' I said.

'And what would I do all day while you're at work? I have my garden to water, my painting to do and my grandchildren to help out with. I'm never lonely, Lachie,' she said.

'What chance have I got against all that?' I said.

Mum's face turned more serious now and she said 'I want you to know that your father was proud of you at the finish and I'm glad he did the right thing by you. He could have left you without a penny. I know he could be an aggressive bore and his attitude to women was terrible, but there were compensations for me, Lachie . . . Like you children, this lovely old house and garden. And Stuart is very kind to me if not to other people,' she said.

'Looks like he's managing the place well,' I said diplomatically.

'Are you still friends with that nice Luke Stirling? I thought Judy was a lovely person,' said Mum, moving on to easier ground.

'Yes, Luke is still my best mate and we still go fishing together. He and Judy helped me a lot with the house after the divorce,' I said. 'Now, are you going to show me your paintings?' I asked.

We spent an enjoyable hour or so looking at the garden and going through some of Mum's more recent paintings, which were very impressive. Her prize-winning painting was particularly good. She'd originally taken up art to distract herself from the pain of Kenneth's death. She put her improvement down to lessons and all the time she had now to devote to her painting.

After we'd thoroughly inspected the paintings Mum showed me some of Vickie's photography. 'She got interested in photography after you sent us some of your shots travelling around Australia. I bought her the camera she took these with and the extra lens to go with it,' said Mum. 'Vickie probably didn't need such an expensive camera but she was very uptight after a row with her father about her desire to get more involved in the management of Kamilaroi. They ended up having a blazing row. She was furious about Stuart's point blank refusal to allow her to show sheep and cattle again. She'd set her heart on doing that when she left college. Stuart seemed to have closed all the avenues to her doing what she was keen to do. And then there's . . .' she started, then hesitated.

'There's . . . ?' I prompted.

'They wouldn't want me to say anything and it's not your problem, Lachie. You've got other matters to worry about,' she said.

'Who are "they" and what isn't my problem?' I asked gently.

'I'll talk to you about it after you finish your work here. You've obviously got some important things to deal with right now and your head shouldn't be cluttered up with other things. What do you think of Vickie's pictures?' she asked.

Looking through the photo album of Vickie's photos, there had been a steady improvement in picture layout with a big jump in quality which must have been after she began using the new camera. A couple that featured the Warrumbungles were especially noteworthy.

'Who took Vickie to the Warrumbungles?' I asked.

'I did, Lachie. Girls Vickie's age shouldn't go to bush places on their own,' she said.

I smiled at that. There were creeps who bashed and raped women older than Mum. She wouldn't have been a deterrent if a bloke wanted to harm Vickie.

'And you needn't smile in that condescending way, Lachie. I still carry a shotgun under the front seat of the car,' she said.

'You could be arrested for that. It's called going armed in public,' I said.

'Don't be so legalistic, Lachie. There's no telling when you might have to use a gun in the country. If it comes to that, I bet you carry one yourself,' she said.

'Yeah, but I have a special dispensation to carry them,' I protested. 'Anyway I was only joking. Mum.'

'That's all right then. Anyway Vickie and I have been up there a few times now. She's a lovely girl and it's unfortunate Stuart can't get his head around a woman helping out with the running of Kamilaroi,' she said. 'It doesn't matter how much Nicole or I talk to him about his sexism, it's just so ingrained in him.'

I had never heard Mum criticise Stuart in such a fashion so matters really must have come to a head. Notwithstanding, it was very pleasant to sit with her and chat about my nieces and nephew as well as things going on around the district and Kamilaroi.

Mum had just started telling me about a friend of hers whose husband had cancer when we heard the sound of a vehicle on the drive. Mum went over to the window and looked out. 'It's Nicole, and Vickie's with her,' she said, her expression suddenly grave.

CHAPTER 14

Nicole and Vickie both stopped dead when they came into the lounge room and saw me. Next thing, Vickie had run over and thrown her arms round my neck and almost strangled me.

'Uncle Lachie, you bad bad person. Why didn't you tell us you were coming?'

'I couldn't, Vickie. I'm up here on a hush-hush work trip. You mustn't let on that you've seen me,' I said.

Vickie stepped back and looked at me with shining eyes. 'But how exciting.' Vickie had a highly coloured idea of the life I led, stemming from her passion for reading all manner of crime novels. She imagined my life as a kind of thrill-a-minute existence.

After a pause Nicole said, 'Lachie, how lovely to see you,' in her soft, throaty voice. Naturally, as someone more experienced in the ways of the world than her daughter, she no doubt guessed that any hush-hush work visit might entail more danger than excitement.

'Nanna's just been showing me some of your photos,' I said to Vickie.

'Oh, Nanna, you shouldn't have. They're not good enough by miles,' said Vickie.

'I've got some great photography gear with me, Vickie,' I told her. 'I bought a 400-mm lens before I left and it makes a big difference, especially for nature photos. When I have some time I'll show you.'

Mum made everyone a cup of tea and brought out a tray of Anzacs. Nicole looked tired and stressed but was her normal warm and friendly self. After a while Mum said she needed to get started on lunch so I shut myself in Father's old office and rang Christine to see if anything had come up I needed to deal with. She assured me that between her and Dasher Doyle everything was running pretty smoothly but gave me a couple of messages from people who'd called in my absence.

When we finished going through the messages and talking through a few things I asked to speak to Dasher. The latter reiterated that apart from one speeding offence, Brewster was clear and there was no record of any Zane Reid.

After putting my mobile away, I considered what Dasher had told me. I wasn't surprised to find that neither Brewster nor Reid had any 'form' though there was a nagging suspicion in my mind that Reid might have a record in the US, so I'd be interested to know what Ballinger turned up about him. In the light of my suspicions about him and Brewster it was possible that the two of them had done some swindling in the jewellery business and things had got too hot for them.

Towards the end of lunch Mum said, 'Vickie, can you please take me down to the village? I need to pick up a few things for dinner now that Lachie's here.'

After they'd left, Nicole and I were quiet for a while, so I decided to raise all the dramas going on with Stuart.

'How are things going for you, Nicole?' I asked.

'Oh, Lachie, I don't know where to begin. The long and short of it is that I've decided to leave Stuart. Things haven't been going well for ages. Marriage to Stuart has never been a bed of roses but I decided a long time ago that I should stay with him for the girls' sake. Now though, I've got to the point where the tension and arguments are outweighing the benefit to the kids of us staying together. A lot of our rows have been about him wanting me to have another baby because he's desperate for a son to take over Kamilaroi.'

I nodded and waited for her to continue.

'Vickie had it in her head that she wanted to have a role in the stud side of things when she left ag college. She wanted to start showing Kamilaroi sheep and cattle again, which Stuart had talked about doing for years. But when she raised it with Stuart he made his usual disparaging remarks about the unsuitability of girls running farming operations. You know what he's like. Even though Vickie and Stuart have never been as close as I'd have liked, Vickie loves so much about farming and she did brilliantly at ag college. Since she came home they've had one row after another.

'The trouble between them came to a head when Vickie told him she'd been offered a job working on the breeding program on a big stud near Quirindi and that she intended to take it. Stuart was furious about her applying for it without his knowledge and said he wouldn't hear of it. Vickie declared that she was going anyway since there was no work for her at Kamilaroi and she wanted to do something with her ag knowledge. Stuart slapped her face and said there was no way he would allow it. Vickie stormed out of the room, took the ute and drove in to Flora's. Stuart went in and brought her back but she refuses to speak to him.

'His attitude to Vickie's farming ambitions was bad enough but the final straw for me was when I found out Stuart had been seeing another woman. She works for one of the agents in Gunnedah but she has a farm and breeds thoroughbreds. I tackled Stuart about it and we had a terrible row that ended in him hitting me,' she said.

'God help me,' I breathed, truly ashamed to have a brother who'd hit a woman, thinking how Nicole had to be some kind of a saint to have stayed with Stuart as long as she had. 'No one will blame you if you decide to leave Stuart,' I said. 'A person can put up with only so much. And there's a limit to the idea of staying together for the children. But what will you do and where will you go?' I asked.

'I don't have any solid plans, Lachie, only a couple of half thought out ideas. But I just have to get out of here before I lose it altogether,' she said. 'There's not much on offer here but I'm scared that if I leave Coonabarabran with the girls Stuart will fight me for custody.'

'How are you off for money, Nicole?' I asked.

'I have a little bit put away but not a lot. Stuart's always handled the money side of things. He gives me cash for shopping but most of the bills are paid by cheque,' she said.

I nodded, sympathetic to what she was saying.

'If I divorce Stuart I guess I'd be entitled to half of his share of Kamilaroi, but it'd probably take a couple of years to settle, what with the kids and all. I've told Stuart if he wants to keep

Shelley and Maureen at private schools he'll have to pay all the fees because there's no way I'd be able to afford to contribute to them. I always wanted to send them to the local school anyway. It's been great for Brett and Katrina.'

'I agree,' I said. Even though I'd enjoyed going away to school because of the freedom it gave me from Father, if I fulfilled my dream of having children I wouldn't want to send them off to school in Sydney during such a formative part of their lives.

'I've spoken to Laurie's solicitor in the past about what would happen if we divorce,' Nicole continued. 'He said a divorce settlement involving me gaining a half share would probably mean Kamilaroi would have to be sold – unless Stuart could give me a cash settlement. He'd have to borrow money to do that. I worry about what your mum will think if I leave. She stayed with your father right to the bitter end so she probably thinks I should stick through these hard times with Stuart, especially as there's the girls to consider,' she said.

'I think Mum might be more understanding than you expect,' I replied. 'She's very fond of you and she knows you've tried your hardest to make your marriage happy. Also, in a few years the girls will have left home. Look, you and Vickie are welcome to live at my house until you sort things out. And the girls could come and stay with you there during their school holidays. If Stuart decides not to keep them at boarding school there are quite a few good local schools around Neutral Bay. I could rent a flat somewhere nearby and help out when you need me but it would just inflame the situation with Stuart if you were actually living with me. The main thing is that you'll have a place to live for a while,' I said.

'That's so generous of you, Lachie, but I wouldn't dream of turning you out of your home,' she said.

'Don't worry about me, Nicole. I'm always so busy I often sleep at the office. I could easily do that until I find somewhere else,' I said.

'Thanks, Lachie, I really appreciate your offer, but I need to have more of a think about things first. I may still stay in Coonabarabran so that the girls can see Stuart when they come home. Also, I like being close to your mum and I'm very close to Flora and Stuart and fond of their kids, and all the cousins are really close too,' she said.

I felt a twinge for my brother, losing his family like this. I couldn't believe he'd been so stupid as to have an affair with someone given how lovely Nicole was. And it wouldn't have hurt him to give Vickie her head and allow her to show sheep and cattle. In fact it'd have been good for Kamilaroi's reputation. It was a pity he had to be so pigheaded. And not only would a divorce be devastating for Nicole and the girls it'd be tough on Mum if they left Coonabarabran altogether.

'What do you think, Lachie? Am I doing the right thing?' Nicole asked, nearly in tears.

My heart went out to her because I had some idea of what she was going through given how wretched I'd been about Fiona's affair and our marriage failing. Even though I realised now that it was for the best that wasn't how I felt at the time. And it would be so much worse with kids involved.

'I'm hardly the right person to ask, Nicole. My marriage failed and I don't have any kids, let alone three. I wouldn't be game to advise you. This has got to be your decision, but my house is definitely there for you if you need it,' I said.

'Thanks again, Lachie,' said Nicole.

'No worries. And just so you know, I may be here for a while depending on how the case I'm working on goes. I'll be staying here tonight and pushing off in the morning after which I'll be incommunicado for a while. Here are the keys to my place in case you do decide to head down to Sydney, even if it's just for a breather and some thinking time. Also, if you need some carry-on money let me know and I'll transfer some funds to you or get my secretary to,' I told her. 'If you do head down there, Flora can get a couple of sets cut for you and Vickie and leave these ones with her.'

When Vickie and Mum got home Nicole took Vickie into another room to talk to her. After a while, Vickie came out and told Mum that Nicole wanted to talk to her too. Mum looked shattered when she and Nicole came back into the kitchen, though Nicole's expression was one of firm resolve. The long and the short of it was that Nicole told Mum she'd decided to accept an offer I'd made to her to use my house in Sydney. She said she needed to get away to think and consider her options but there was a chance she'd come back to Coonabarabran.

I felt very sorry for Mum, who looked stricken. All this was very traumatic for her. My marriage had been a failure and now she was about to witness the disintegration of Stuart's marriage and the break-up of his family. But, as always, her thoughts were on others and she asked Vickie if she'd like to make some shortbread with her.

After they went off to the kitchen Nicole said there was no way she'd accept my hospitality without paying me some rent and that she'd look for a temp job when she got down to Sydney. She ignored my protestations that rent was totally unnecessary and asked me for some recommendations re employment agencies. I suggested she get in contact with Christine because she knew everyone and was bound to be able to help both her and Vickie find some temporary work.

Nicole thanked me again and then breathed a huge sigh and said it was time for her to go and talk to Stuart. I gave her an encouraging hug and wished her luck.

Just before dark Nicole returned, her eyes red from crying. She was too distressed to talk when she arrived so Mum took her into the spare bedroom and closed the door. Some women would have been angry with their daughter-in-law in such a situation but Mum loved Nicole and had a lot of sympathy for her.

Outside, the back seat of Nicole's car was piled high with suitcases and boxes.

'She's finally done it,' said Vickie as I walked back into the lounge. 'I wasn't sure she'd go through with it,' said Vickie.

'It's a big step, Vickie. Your mother's spent over half her life with your father. Now she has to more or less start all over again,' I said.

'If Dad wasn't so pig-headed and controlling of us all, this would never have happened,' said Vickie angrily.

'He's not entirely to blame for the way he is, Vickie. Our father was harsh with us all but he put a lot of his expectations on your dad in particular because he was the eldest. Your dad learned to second-guess our father and was always trying to please him. If we'd had a different kind of father, your own dad might have turned out differently. I have some sympathy for him,' I said.

'Do you think I'm being selfish and unreasonable to leave Kamilaroi?' she asked.

'Not if you find it impossible to come to terms with your father,' I replied.

'The sad thing is that I'm sure I could have done as well as any boy at Kamilaroi and he wouldn't give me a go,' said Vickie sadly.

CHAPTER 15

I wondered how long it would take before Stuart put in an appearance. It was probably too late in the evening for him to come over, particularly given he'd probably need to talk to the woman he was carrying on with about what was going on. It turned out that he arrived during breakfast and started mouthing off as soon as he came through the door.

'This is all your fault, you bastard,' he shouted at me. 'We don't see you for three years and after only one day back you've turned everything upside down. This family's never been the same since you blamed Father for Kenneth's death. And though he never recovered from your slur on him he was big enough to leave you a third share of Kamilaroi – and that's despite you not lifting a finger around here since you left. And as if that wasn't bad enough, you're now actively involved in breaking up my family.'

'Sit down and shut up, Stuart,' I said. 'Let me assure you that until I arrived here I had very little idea of what was going on with you and your family. I've had nothing to do with Nicole's decision to leave you, though I think she deserves a medal for not doing it years ago. And Vickie's not going to hang around while you aren't prepared to give her a proper job here. You're so much like Father. And we all know about your other woman so don't complain that *you've* been treated badly,' I said.

Although he turned very red in the face with fury it was clear he was also devastated by what was going on and I felt a pang of sympathy for him.

'I didn't come here to pick a fight with you, Stuart. Nicole and Vickie are leaving here and their futures are more important to me than anything else that's going on here. You had your chance to keep Vickie and you turned her down. And the affair you're having would be reason for any woman to leave you quite apart from your patronising, bullying behaviour. You're in a lot of trouble, Stuart. Nicole will be entitled to half your share of Kamilaroi if she divorces you – and no one would blame her if she did given your shenanigans. Now clear out and allow me to finish my breakfast in peace,' I said.

Stuart's face changed from red to white before he turned and stomped out of the kitchen. Mum followed him out looking terribly distressed but Vickie came over and hugged me. Nicole looked slightly dazed.

I went outside to ring Flora on my mobile and related the whole sorry story, adding that Nicole had accepted an offer I'd made for her and Vickie to head down to Sydney and stay in my house down there. Flora said that was a good idea and asked if she could speak with Nicole. Heading back inside I handed the phone over to Nicole, explaining that it was Flora. She took the phone outside and spoke to Flora for a good long time and when she came inside she looked considerably better and said she and Vickie were going to spend a day or two with Flora before driving to Sydney.

Mum and I hugged Nicole and Vickie and waved them off, Mum holding off on the tears till we got back inside and broke down. I comforted her as much as I could and we talked for a while about what was going on with Stuart. I suggested she visit him to see how he was getting on, maybe even stay the night, which she thought was a good idea. Like any loving mother, she was worried about how he would cope. She went off to pack a few things in case she stayed the night at Stuart's and we both left at the same time. I kissed her goodbye before I got in my car and promised I'd be out again soon.

Given how upset Mum had been I'd decided against asking her if she could go into town to fill up my car with petrol, which I'd been hoping she could do to avoid anyone seeing me. Instead I put on my dark glasses and Akubra and fervently hoped I wouldn't bump into anyone I knew. It was a risk to go anywhere too close to Coonabarabran but I needed petrol so I had no choice.

I stopped to fill up at the petrol station furthest from town, which is when I spotted a creepy looking old sod with longish, greasy mousey-going-grey hair. Slightly stooped and wearing shabby clothes, there was something familiar about him. When I went inside the station to pay for my petrol he was just leaving the till. After he'd gone outside I casually asked the attendant who he was. My heart thudded when he said it was 'that old bastard Challis'. I looked out just in time to see Challis get into a mud-streaked cream Holden utility with a green tarpaulin covering the back tray. Just as I was pretending to key in a phone number but actually noting down the ute's rego my mobile phone rang.

It was Morris, who said. 'Your package is coming in tomorrow. By air. I'll meet the plane. You're to be at the station at eleven.'

'Will do and thanks for that. Do you mind checking this rego out for me,' I said as the cream utility disappeared into the distance.

'Another development?' he asked.

'It's always handy to know who owns a particular vehicle. You sometimes find them in awfully strange places,' I said. 'Any chance you could text me the name of the owner of the vehicle?'

'Sure,' said Morris. 'What are you up to next?'

'I'm heading out to have a look at the Gorge so I can work out the possibilities,' I said.

'For God's sake be careful,' said Morris.

'Don't worry, I will. Talk soon,' I said.

CHAPTER 16

There were several hours of daylight left for me to have a good look around the Gorge, suss out the logistics of the location in relation to the Challis and Brewster properties, and work out the best place to camp. Looking at my map, I suspected camping somewhere near the rock pool would probably be a good idea given both the access to water and because it was adjacent to the road that led up to the Brewster and Challis properties. Though Milson had said both properties were fairly well cleared they backed on to some very thick timber and rocky ridges.

Travelling out to the Gorge involved taking a gravel track that turned south-west off the Baradine Road to the north of the Warrumbungles. After turning off the Baradine Road, I drove through a thickly pined area before arriving at the Gorge – so named because over millions of years a narrow creek had carved out a kind of cutting in a rocky outcrop. At the base of this rocky outcrop was the rock pool, which was about fifty metres long. Beyond the pool and the rocky outcrop, the ground sloped upwards for about three-quarters of a kilometre to a high ridge that dominated the immediate area. Looking up at it I noted it would provide a good view of the rock pool and where I'd be camping.

The gravel road I'd driven in on continued beyond the camping area, forking about three hundred metres beyond the rock pool where there were two mail boxes, one wooden and one made from a big kerosene tin. I took a casual stroll up there with my camera as if looking for things to photograph and saw that the name Brewster was printed on the wooden one and there was a barely legible Challis on the kero tin. A steel gate spanned the road a small distance beyond these mail boxes. The left hand fork disappeared into dense pine country and I noticed there was a telephone line to the Brewster property.

I set up my 400-mm lens on a tripod and had a good look at the ridge. I then gathered some dry sticks and soon had a small fire to boil my billy. There were birds singing and twittering all around me as I tucked into my food so I decided I'd actually do a serious spot of photography while I was here.

As the sun disappeared behind the clouds the reserve suddenly felt a little spooky. There were no houses in sight and the camping area was enclosed completely by pines and low scrub, making me wonder how a policewoman from Sydney would cope here, even one chosen for her experience with firearms and in dangerous situations.

I decided to take a walk along the creek to look for koalas in the adjacent gums and had a stroke of luck when I found koala droppings underneath a big scribbly gum. Peering up, I spied two koalas in the tree about fifteen metres above the ground. Using another camera with a 200-mm lens I snapped off what I thought might be passable pics of them. My next big break was spying a Regent Honey-eater in a nearby tree. I hurried back to get the big lens and managed to get a couple of pics of it.

By the time night fell there'd been no sign of any activity on the ridge and no movement to or from either the Challis or Brewster properties. Satisfied with my day's photography, I packed up and drove back to town where I called in on Flora to see how Nicole and Vickie were taking their first night away from Kamilaroi.

'How are they?' I asked Flora.

'Vickie is fine because she's hanging out with the kids. Nicole is in a bit of a daze,' said Flora. 'Mum rang to say she's staying the night at Stuart's because he's very down.'

'That's totally understandable,' I said. 'He and Nicole have been married a lot longer than me and I was terribly upset when Fiona and I split. And she'll be worried about the girls too. Thank goodness Fiona and I didn't have children to complicate things.'

'Do you want to stay here tonight?' Flora asked.

'If you've got a spare bed,' I said. 'Mum's at Stuart's and it'd be good to go through a few things about my house with Nicole. Tomorrow I go bush and it'll be much harder to make contact with anyone.'

'You'll be careful, won't you?' she said.

'It's my middle name, Flora,' I said.

'That's a laugh!' said Flora, snorting. 'If only it'd been your middle name when you took that bullet. Does the wound still give you any trouble?'

'Nah, it's as good as gold,' I said.

'I hate to think of you out in the bush on your own,' she said.

'I'll have an undercover police officer with me from tomorrow,' I replied, neglecting to tell her that the police officer would be female.

'Oh, thank goodness,' she said with obvious relief.

Nicole thanked me again for letting me use her house and gave me my keys back, since she'd had a couple of sets cut. It was clear she was apprehensive about the future and her place in it. Even though she'd been thinking of leaving Stuart for a long time she was still aware that going solo was going to take a lot of adjustment.

'There are better times ahead, Nicole. I guarantee it. Based on what I went through it's best to take every day as it comes. After a while, you'll be surprised at how much happier you feel,' I said, keen to reassure her.

'I hope you're right. I feel incredibly confused. Even though I know in my heart I'm doing the right thing, it's still a wrench and I still worry about whether separating from Stuart will be bad for the girls. I also worry about your mother because she's always been so wonderful to me. And she loves all the girls. Then again, it'll be good to be in Sydney so I can see more of the girls. They'll love being day students and spending more time at home.'

'Of course they will. You'll probably have to share them with Stuart but before long Shelley and Maureen will be old enough to make their own decisions,' I said. 'All the girls are great kids and a credit to you and Stuart.'

CHAPTER 17

As I walked into Coonabarabran police station early the next morning Les Milson handed me a fax from Superintendent Ballinger:

To LR

I'm sending you my niece Detective-Senior Constable Gaye Walker. She's a very competent officer. Gaye is fully aware of the risks posed by this assignment. She's in your hands and I know you'll look after her to the best of your ability. She'll follow your instructions unless they transgress police and legal guidelines.

Good luck

Ballinger

Ps Luke Stirling caught a 17 lb dusky flathead off Wagstaff.

I knew a little about Gaye Walker via the police grapevine. She'd worked in the Vice Squad for a while before moving to homicide, where she was highly respected.

'You're to go through,' Milson said when I'd finished reading the fax. I thanked him, and walked down the passage before entering Morris's office. And there was Gaye, talking to Morris.

'Lachie, I'd like you to meet Detective Senior Constable Gaye Walker,' said Morris.

She stood up and put out her hand. Her handshake was firm and cool. She was about five foot ten and looked like a fit and healthy outdoorsy type, which made her perfect for the role she needed to play. 'What would you like me to call you?' she asked, smiling and looking me straight in the eye.

'Just call me Lachie unless we're in company and then maybe you could call me "hon" or "darling" or whatever you think,' I said, smiling back at her. 'The main thing is that I look like a nature photographer and we look like we're very happy together.'

'Sure,' said Gaye.

'We're going into what might be a very high risk situation and to start with there'll only be the two of us,' I said. 'Do you feel comfortable with that?'

'Yep, I'm fine about it,' she said without hesitation. 'Uncle Dick gave me a thorough lowdown on what's expected of me.'

'Okay,' I said before bringing her up to date with what I'd discovered up to this point. When I thought I'd covered everything I possibly could I asked her if she had any questions.

'No, hon,' she said, with a twinkle in her eye.

I laughed and handed her a list and a wad of money. 'Do you mind driving my car to the supermarket and buying all the things on this list. If there're any extra food items you'd like, get them too. I would have done it myself except I come from around here and I'm trying to keep as low a profile as possible.'

'No worries. Uncle Dick told me your family have been up here for generations,' she said, then got up to go.

'As soon as you're back, we'll head out to the Gorge. Meanwhile I'll go over a few things with the sergeant,' I said.

After she left I asked Morris if he'd got around to checking the rego of the ute I'd seen.

'Yep, it's registered to old man Challis,' he said.

'I thought it might be,' I said. 'Is the old fellow a bit stooped with longish, greying hair?'

'That's him,' he said.

'I thought so,' I replied. 'Have you had any info on Reid?'

'Not a thing so far,' said Morris.

This gelled with what Dasher had told me. 'Ten to one he entered the country illegally or used a different name and passport. Nothing from America for Reid?'

'A big zero,' said Morris.

'I wouldn't be surprised if it was Reid who shot the teller. I've got a bad feeling about him. It'd be great if you could line up a medic and an ambulance in case we locate Caroline. If we do, do you think it'd be possible for your guys to block Baradine Road at the turn-off to the Gorge and prevent anyone from entering or leaving it? And it'd probably be worth confiscating all mobile phones. There's at least one more property down the left fork of the road that goes to the Brewster and Challis properties and we don't know whether the owner of this property is a crook or not. His name is Costigan. Can you get Senior Constable Milson's opinion about this fellow? I'll aim to ring in tomorrow morning and whenever I can after that,' I said.

'I'll get Milson on to finding out about Costigan,' said Morris. 'And if you need our help in confronting those bastards all you have to do is give me the word,' he added. 'If you want a man or men, get straight on to me.'

'Thanks, Ming. If we find Caroline Clemenger you can rest assured I'll be straight on to you. The only issue might be mobile phone reception in some of the places out there. I'm going to walk around a bit to see where the mobile reception is best. It was patchy in the Gorge and it could be non-existent on the Brewster and Challis places. There's a highish ridge at the Gorge that concerns me a little.

'Ah, yes, mobile reception can get pretty patchy once you leave the outskirts of town,' Ming conceded.

'If my hunch is right and Caroline Clemenger is being held at the Challis farm I'll be aiming to try and neutralise whoever's guarding her without alarming Brewster or Reid. If we can get Caroline away I'll be calling you guys wherever I can find mobile reception so you can go in and grab the lot of them. Apart from praying she's still alive, I'm hoping that Brewster, Reid and Ted Challis aren't all there, but I'm not banking on it,' I said.

Gaye returned in about forty minutes with all the things on the list, plus a few more.

'Before we head off I want to show you some photos,' I said and passed her the prints of Caroline Clemenger and Ted Challis. 'That's the woman they abducted and that's the fellow the police think drove the getaway vehicle at the ANC bank job she was abducted during. He's not the brains of the bunch and they may have involved him because he'd had experience driving fast cars.'

Gaye had a good long look at both the pictures and then handed them back to me.

'Got them in your head?' I asked.

She nodded.

'Did Ballinger give you any instructions?' I asked.

'Yes, that I'm to act as if you're my boyfriend and follow your instructions to the letter unless I consider them to be prejudicial to the good name of the police force. I'm not to shoot at anyone unless there's no alternative. He also said that if there are arrests to be made, I have to make them because you're no longer in the Force,' she said.

'That's right, but I need you to know I'm worried the situation we're going into is even more dangerous than I originally thought because there may be more men involved than Brewster, Reid and Ted Challis,' I said before explaining why I thought Caroline Clemenger was being held and my hunch that she was being guarded by one or more of the Challis bunch. 'I have a feeling Brewster and Reid aren't the kind of blokes who'd want to be saddled with a female prisoner. We've got evidence they've been to the races a couple of times since the heist so they probably want to be free to come and go. Also, Ted Challis has been keeping a very low profile.

'With all I've now told you I wouldn't blame you a bit if you wanted to pull out. Now's the time to do so if you're of that mind,' I said.

'There's no way I want to bail,' said Gaye. 'In fact I'm keener than ever to get started.'

'That's great, then let's get this show on the road,' I said, relieved that all the information I'd given her had neither impacted on her decision to continue nor dented her composure.

'Have you decided where we're going to camp?' Gaye asked after we'd farewelled Morris and were heading out to the car.

'I went out to the Gorge yesterday and found a great spot. It's quite a beautiful place with a rock pool and a good vantage point to try and work out what's going on. The track up to the Brewster and Challis properties goes right past the pool and the camping site I've chosen. By the way, where's your Browning?' I asked.

She indicated a holster in the waistband of her shorts and told me it was already loaded.

'Great,' I said. 'I've got mine holstered on my waist too. At night you should keep it under your pillow.'

On the way out to the Gorge we started making more detailed plans for the operation we were on.

'The way I see it is that we'll get set up with a tent and my hide to establish that we're there to do some serious wildlife photography. I'll have to leave you at the camp while I scout up around the ridge. If Caroline is at either the Challis or Brewster properties – and I suspect if she's still alive she'll be at the Challis farm – we'll have to assess whether we can remove her and how we should do it. The numbers of people possibly with her have become more of a concern for me. We're likely to be outnumbered and therefore out-gunned. If the job looks too risky, we'll have to utilise Ming and his men,' I said. But it's very much a suck-it-and-see situation. Do you agree?' I asked.

'I agree. I haven't seen the lie of the land and until I do I can't really envisage what you've got in mind. What I do understand, though, is that there are men who are probably in two places and that you think Caroline is being held at the Challis farm. If that proves to be the case you want to remove her and then let Sergeant Morris deal with Brewster and Company. In other words, you don't want a war on two fronts,' she said.

'That's exactly what I think,' I said, pleased at how clearly she saw things and the calm, logical way she operated. 'But we'll have to play it by ear and see how things work out. You know as well as I do that things don't always work out the way you hope, so the planning and execution are all important.'

'Yeah. Especially when the particular criminals involved are feeling desperate,' she said.

We didn't speak again until the turn-off to the Gorge came up on the left. I stopped the vehicle and we looked around at the extent of the timber and scrub all around us. 'That's where the cavalry will have to be if and when we need them,' I said. 'From this point on we're entering no-man's-land, Gaye. There's a high possibility that Caroline is being held down there,' I said pointing in the direction of the Challis place.

Now that we were here, it was easier to talk about the logistics of the operation. 'This is the only road in to the Brewster and Challis properties. What goes up this road has to come back out this same road. There may be tracks through the scrub but there are no other roads a vehicle can use. However, if any of these fellows get away into the scrub we can kiss them goodbye and it will be a police manhunt,' I said.

'What makes you think Caroline Clemenger is here?' asked Gaye.

'I have an utterly reliable source regarding a sighting of her in Coonabarabran and that's been the strongest lead about where she is so far. And then there's the fact that the crook who drove the getaway car is a Challis from here. I'm just hoping Caroline's still alive. Two months is a fair spell for a woman to spend with a bunch of crooks ,' I said, then started the car again and continued driving. Almost immediately the pines closed in on us.

'It's kind of spooky,' said Gaye. 'It's like the trees are hemming us in,' she said.

'It will improve when we get to the Gorge. But you're right, and it's spooky as hell once the sun goes down. There are lots of places in the Pilliga where you could get lost quite easily. If the Pilliga could talk, God alone knows what it might reveal,' I said.

We drove through a tunnel of pines for about two kilometres before we came to the rock pool and camping area. I pulled over towards the creek and pointed the vehicle back towards the exit to the Gorge reserve. After we got out, Gaye acted the adoring girlfriend as we looked around the site, me pointing out birds and where the koalas were.

'Where are the two homesteads?' Gaye murmured.

'You can't see either of them from here. They're on the other side of that ridge. How far I can't tell you but I wouldn't think they'd be too far,' I said. 'Once I get my camera out we can go for a bit of a walk under the guise of taking some photos and I can point out various things to you.'

We unloaded the vehicle and I pitched the tent beside the rock pool with the opening pointing up towards the ridge. I used a big roll of canvas I'd brought to cover the vehicle and form a kind of annexe between it and the tent so we could move between them without being seen.

'You take the tent. It's a state-of-the-art number that Mrs Kendall bought for me and will be very comfortable,' I said. 'I'll sleep in the car.'

'Thanks, but shouldn't we both sleep in the tent given that we're supposed to be girlfriend and boyfriend?' she asked.

'I didn't want to put you in an uncomfortable situation by suggesting that,' I said, 'but it might be good given that we'll take turns to go into the hide to keep a lookout while the other sleeps.'

Gaye pitched in very well and in no time at all we had the camp set up. Gaye was clearly very practical and level-headed and didn't seem at all fazed by being alone with me in the bush.

'Tea or coffee?' I asked as the billy came to the boil.

'Tea for preference. I was bush-reared. Be back in a moment,' she said, opening the flap onto the tent and going inside.

When Gaye emerged from the tent she'd changed into short shorts and a halter top and looked perfect for the role of outdoorsy girlfriend.

'Is this what you had in mind for how I should dress to look believable?' she asked.

'It couldn't be better,' I said. 'There's your tea.'

'What are we going to do now?' she asked.

'I'm going to set up my hide for photographing birds and animals so it's in place before anyone comes past. They're bound to come right up close to it in order to suss things out. Then I'll set up a tripod and mount a camera. You got the Browning in place?' I asked.

She nodded and touched her waist.

I built the framework of my hide with tubular aluminium. The hessian covering was attached by cords to the frame and the whole contraption was very light and could be shifted quite easily. I set it up with two of its apertures facing the road and the ridge. You could sit in it with the long 400 mm pointing through either aperture or use binoculars to search for suitable subjects for 'shooting'.

From inside I used my binoculars to check out the ridge but there was no sign of life there.

I gestured to Gaye to hold my hand so we were in character and we walked down the creek a little way until we came to a couple of scribbly gums. The two koalas were still in the same tree they'd been sleeping in the previous day, though they were higher up now.

'Look up there,' I told Gaye, pointing towards where they were.

'Oh, hon, I've never seen koalas outside a park,' she said.

'I took a couple of shots of them yesterday but they were too sleepy for good pictures. You'll probably hear them grunting tonight. They can make quite a racket.'

Gaye looked up and down the creek and then looked at me. 'It seems a very unlikely place to find big-time crims. I'm more used to staking them out in flashy places like King's Cross.'

'Both Brewster and Challis have long-standing connections with this area which is why I think we'll find them around here somewhere. If Caroline's being held at the Challises, then she'll be in that direction,' I said, carefully indicating the direction of their place with my head – that's if she isn't dead and buried in the scrub somewhere. Milson told me the Challis house is the second place behind the ridge. Brewster's is the first,' I said. 'We'll have to put in tomorrow establishing our credentials because there's a good chance they'll come by to check us out reasonably quickly,' I told her.

'Okay,' said Gaye, her expression suddenly serious.

'This is a get in and get out quickly operation,' I said. 'We can't afford to be seen moseying up the road to inspect the countryside. It would make them instantly suspicious. Posing as a wildlife photographer is the only avenue I could think of that would legitimately allow us to get so close to the places over the ridge. Having done that I'll go round by the ridge and have a look-see at what's doing.'

I put some crushed ice in a bucket and buried a bottle of Riesling and a couple of stubbies in it. 'Take your pick,' I said.

We talked more about what we'd need to do and possible outcomes over the next hour till we both felt confident. Then I asked Gaye if she could take both our phones for a bit of a walk to see where the best reception was in case we sent for reinforcements. After she came back she pointed out a few places.

Towards evening the bird population increased markedly. There were birds singing and twittering all around the pool as well as up and down the creek.

'Keep an eye out for black cockatoos,' I said, pulling out my bird book and showing her some photos of them. 'Red-tailed Black Cockatoos specifically,' I added, pointing to a picture of one. 'They're definitely to be found in the Pilliga and the water ought to attract them here. And given we're here I'd like to get some shots of them.'

'Sure,' she said and we set off on a black cockatoo scouting expedition, again keeping an eye on our phones for the places with the best mobile reception.

'How come you joined the police force?' I asked as we walked towards the ridge.

'It seemed the best option and nothing else really jumped at me. I admired the police and the job they do and I was very fond of Uncle Dick. He said I could apply to be in the mounted police and move on from there. So I did and then after a few years I applied to go into Vice and then later I applied for the Homicide division. Over the last few years I've decided I don't want to be a cop forever. I wouldn't mind making sergeant and then considering my options. What I'd really like to do is get back to the bush so I can breed some good horses. I like working cattle with horses like my dad did when I was younger,' she said.

'I know what you mean,' I said. 'If I could do anything I wanted I'd buy a property with a long, meandering tree-lined creek running through it where cattle could lie in the shade and chew their cuds while they stack on the beef. I sometimes dream about living in a homestead with big wide verandahs like the one I grew up in, though I didn't think I'd ever be able to afford anything as lavish as it. I loved growing up on a property and I want any kids I might have to enjoy the same sort of upbringing, with lots of open spaces to explore and ponies to ride, and a feel for the changing seasons.'

'How will you get on if your wife doesn't want to live in the bush?' she asked.

'Now that I'm older and wiser I think it's important for husbands and wives to share dreams so I probably wouldn't have a relationship with someone who wasn't interested in ever moving to the country. I don't know if your Uncle Dick told you, but my ex-wife, Fiona, turned out to be a real city girl with no interest in moving back to the country. She loved being a doctor but she had no desire to have a practice in a country town,' I said.

'If I loved a man enough to marry him I'd like it to be a lifetime commitment,' she said. 'I think a marriage break-up is very unfair on children.'

'Very unfair,' I agreed. 'Do you have a boyfriend?'

She shook her head. 'Not at the moment.'

'Where did you grow up?' I asked.

'We had a place in the Monaro. Mum was mad about horses and we spent hours riding together. She had a freak accident while she was riding one day and died instantly. Dad started to drink too much after that and was DUI when he was killed in a car accident,' she said. 'Uncle Dick became my guardian after Dad's death and he and Aunty Gaye were great to me. Despite the way Mum died, Uncle Dick encouraged me to keep riding because he thought it was important. They used to take me back to the Monaro for my holidays and I still love it there.'

We talked for a while about the different country areas we both liked and then Gaye said she was tired. I suggested she have the first sleep while I kept a lookout for any visitors. She agreed but insisted I wake her at 2 so I could get some sleep too. She then helped me to rig up a fishing line with some tins so we could yank it to wake each other up if anyone appeared. The whole contraption was virtually invisible by torchlight and we could roll it up in the morning. It wasn't full moonlight, maybe three parts full, so if anyone came in off the road I could get behind them quite easily from the hide.

CHAPTER 18

Apart from the koalas and the mopoke, it was a very quiet night, the only sound from beyond the ridge the soft putt-putt of a generator. Clearly, bulk electricity hadn't been laid on to this section of the scrub so all the farms here would be dependent on generators.

At 2 a.m. Gaye took over the hide and I lay down and got to sleep very quickly.

I woke early and Gaye and I carted all the gear back to the vehicle, then rolled up the fishing line and hid it and the empty tins under a shrub. There was plenty of firewood close by and I soon had a fire going and the billy bubbling. We were just finishing our breakfast when a pair of Red-tailed Black Cockatoos alighted on the top of one of the scribbly gums.

Rushing to the hide, I adjusted the tripod and focused on the two cockies. They were a pair because the female cockie had orange-yellow tail feathers rather than the red of the male. I got out one of my bird books and did a bit of study on the various cockatoos and on some of the other birds of the Pilliga area.

'What's the plan for the day?' Gaye asked.

'If the blokes over that ridge respond to our smoke we'll have visitors down here this morning. They'll give us the once over and decide whether we're genuine campers or not. Judging by the ashes, there've been other campers here quite recently so we shouldn't come across as suspicious,' I said.

'What then?' Gaye asked.

'If I sight them peeking at us from the ridge I'll ask you to change into your bikini outfit and have a splash in the pool. I'll take a couple of pictures of you and then I'll pick you up and take you across to the tent. That ought to convince them we're genuine partners. When they've gone and after we've had a quick lunch, I'll head out for the top of the ridge and see if I can sight Caroline. You'll have to mind the camp while I'm gone. That's what I've got in mind if everything falls into place. Does that all sound alright to you?' I asked.

'I'd prefer to go with you to the ridge. Two people are better than one in an emergency,' Gaye said.

'It wouldn't be a good idea to leave this camp unattended and I couldn't risk sending you alone into uncharted waters, so to speak. Ballinger would have my guts for garters. If Caroline Clemenger is over that ridge you'll get your chance tomorrow,' I said.

I threw a couple more leafy green branches on the fire and watched as the dark smoke climbed skyward in the still air. It was time we smoked out the blokes over the ridge.

We sat at the table and talked for a few minutes and then Gaye washed some clothes and hung them on the makeshift clothesline to add a touch of domesticity.

'Got your weapon in place?' I asked Gaye.

'Yes, hon,' she said with a grin on her face.

'It might be an idea for you to sit at the table and look at some of those magazines you bought and I'll keep a watch from the hide. I might be able to sneak in a bird pic or two while I'm there.'

While Gaye sat and pretended to read magazines, I continued to watch the ridge through the state-of-the-art binoculars Eunice Kendall had provided. Sure enough, shortly after 10 a.m. two men appeared on the ridge, one carrying a rifle, the other binoculars.

My heart thumped. This was it. I walked over and hugged Gaye, whispering to her about the two blokes and said, 'Can you please go to the tent and get your towel, then take it across to the hide, wrap my binoculars in it, take them back to the tent and then bring yourself and the towel back here. Saunter, Gaye, saunter. Just do it naturally. Don't hurry.'

I went to the vehicle and got out my oldest Nikon with standard lens and hung it around my neck. Then I put on a green, peaked cap and strolled back to the table. Gaye walked back to me carrying her towel and looking tense but resolved. The next few minutes would be critical. If the watchers on the ridge could be convinced that Gaye and me were a dinky di pair of lovers and were content to leave us alone, I could scout off and look for Caroline Clemenger.

'What now, Lachie?' she asked.

'I want you to change into your bikini and then run out into the pool and have a good old splash. I'll take a couple of pics of you before you walk out of the pool. I'll throw you your towel so you can dry yourself. Then I'll pick you up and carry you across to the tent. Act naturally, Gaye,' I said as calmly as I could manage.

A vision in a yellow bikini ran past me and plunged into the rock pool then swam around for several minutes before she emerged and posed for me.

'You've done well, Gaye,' I whispered in her ear before lifting her up in a very boyfriend-like way and carrying her across to the tent and going in with her as if to have some nooky.

'You know what they'll be thinking, don't you?' she asked.

'That's what I want them to think. Sorry, but it's an integral part of the plan. Quick, hand me the binoculars,' I said.

I focused the binoculars on the ridge while behind me Gaye divested herself of her bikini and changed back into her shorts and halter top. Only the bloke with the binoculars was there now.

'We'll have to wait here a while to make it thoroughly convincing,' I told her.

When I next looked up at the ridge the skyline was bare. 'I think we've fooled them,' I said. 'I wonder how long we'll have to wait for our first visitors,' I said and glanced down at my wrist watch. 'I reckon about an hour.'

When we emerged from the tent a few minutes later the day seemed suddenly brighter. 'Let's get this set up. I'll go and get the billy boiling. You put on your sunglasses and hat and sit at the table again. When you talk to me don't forget to lay it on a bit. And move your chair so it and you are facing the road. I'll be in the hide pretending to take pictures when they come so call me,' I told her.

She nodded and then proceeded to do all the things I'd asked of her.

Within half an hour we heard a vehicle coming down the road

from over the ridge and I disappeared into the hide. Gaye sat at the table leafing through a magazine, looking up nonchalantly when the old cream Holden utility pulled up close to my four-wheel drive. Two blokes got out of the ute and I reckoned they were the same two I'd watched on the ridge. They were very alike and they were both wearing rough bush clothes and old, wide-brimmed hats.

'Hello there,' Gaye greeted them. 'Darling, we've got visitors. Imagine that, all the way out here.'

I crawled out of the hide with a big friendly smile on my face, my old Nikon slung about my neck.

'G'day,' I greeted them. 'Amazing place for taking pics of the local wildlife. You live around here?'

'Yep,' said one of them. 'I'm Ted Challis and this is me brother, Jack. Our family live in a place over that ridge.'

I shook hands with them. 'Laurie Rivers, and this is my partner, Gaye. Got a place, eh? What do you run, Ted?' I asked.

'Cattle mostly. We tried sheep but they didn't do well here,' Ted answered.

The brothers Challis were men of medium height with mid-brown hair

'We're not on your land, are we? The tourist people in Coona-barabran told us this was a national parks reserve,' I said.

'It is until you come to a gate and fence up the road a bit,' Jack Challis said.

'If you're locals, maybe you can help me. I'm looking for black cockatoos, the ones with the red tails . . . these fellows,' I said and shoved my bird book across the table towards him. 'You see any of these around here?'

'Nah. You'd want to try the river country for them. I've never seen any here,' he said.

'That's a shame. The tourist people told me they thought I'd have a good chance of seeing some along this creek,' I said.

'Nup, don't think so,' said Jack. 'How long are ya stayin'.'

'We might give it another day. Probably pull up stakes tomorrow. There's koalas here and plenty of other birds. Koala pics are always good value so it won't be a wasted trip. We'll move on then and try a couple of other spots,' I said.

'What's that?' Ted asked and pointed to the hide.

'It's a hide. Nearly all wildlife photographers use a hide. It allows you to get much closer to both birds and animals. Most birds are small and even with a big telephoto lens, you shouldn't be too far away to get good pictures,' I explained. 'Want a cuppa?' I asked.

'Nah, we better be gettin' back. Got things to do. You've got to watch out for fires around here. Some campers are bloody careless and these pines explode like bombs,' said Ted.

'Nice job. Take you anywhere,' said Ted gesturing towards my four-wheel drive as he and his brother walked back to their ute.

'Yeah, it's a real beauty', I said.

Gaye and I waved them a goodbye as Ted turned the vehicle and drove back up the hill.

Once they'd disappeared completely Gaye bent over the table in hysterics. 'Oh, Lachie, that was priceless. You're a real bullshit artist,' she gasped between bursts of laughter.

I laughed too and then turned serious.

'That's the first lot of callers out of the way. The next lot will be tougher,' I said. 'The Challis brothers are only the Indians. They were sent down on a preliminary scouting mission. We may have allayed their suspicions but the real crooks'll look us over anyway. They'll probably leave it until tomorrow morning so they don't look too suspicious but I bet they'll come over and check out if we've headed off. Meanwhile, if you're agreeable I'll head off and see how the land lies over that ridge. Those fellows won't be expecting anyone so soon after their visit.'

Gaye clearly wasn't happy about staying in the camp. Both her personality and police training meant she'd want to be where the action was – and not only that but she'd already said that two people were better than one if something arose.

'Look, I understand that you want to come with me and I'd like to take you but it makes better sense for you to stay here so we don't leave the camp unattended,' I said. 'Sling my old camera round your neck and plant yourself in the scrub by the creek. If anyone stops and starts nosing about, walk out of the scrub and ask them what they want. You can say you were photographing koalas.'

'Okay. Good luck, Lachie,' she said as I set off.

I didn't like leaving her because although she was a police officer and armed, it was a potentially dangerous place. But I had to try and work out exactly where Caroline Clemenger was being held. I didn't want Gaye with me until I was familiar with the set-up over the ridge.

The creek wasn't much more than knee-deep beside our camp. But after leaving it I plunged into a belt of thick pine forest. It was very quiet in amongst the pines and for a little while there was no vision at all. I cast well out into the pines so that I wouldn't hit the ridge head-on because my aim was to come out as far as possible from our side of the ridge.

The ridge tapered away at both ends and was really more of a low hill than part of a continuous ridge. The actual area of elevated ridge was only about half a kilometre long.

After I'd been walking for about twenty minutes I hit the creek again, soon after it forked and became two creeks at my end of the ridge. The other end of the ridge finished near the track up to the Brewster and Challis properties. One arm of the creek turned sharply and was running at almost a right angle to me. For about fifty metres on both sides of this arm, the trees had been almost completely cleared. It was like a great open gash against the darkness and the thickness of the pines. The creek was cleared for a distance of about two kilometres and there were black and red cattle grazing along this stretch of cleared country. It would be a great place to dump stolen stock. No doubt there was a set of cattle yards somewhere in there amongst the pines. Any hint of a police raid and someone would slip away and drive the cattle off the cleared creek country and into either the security of the forest or a well hidden set of yards.

The pines thinned out a little near the end of the ridge and I came to a fence that led back into the pines and it was anchored by a massive post that was bolted to the rock wall of the ridge. Then, drilled out of the ridge was a big opening that was supported by steel trusses and blocked by a steel gate disguised by green pine branches. These were probably replaced as they wilted but there was an endless supply of them so that wouldn't present a problem. On the other side of it was another fence and it was anchored in the same way as the fence on my side. Stolen cattle could easily be trucked up to this disguised gate and liberated into the cleared creek paddock. The left hand fork of the creek turned sharply left and veered away from me in the general direction of where I thought the Challis dwelling would be.

I became ultra cautious now, climbing up the ridge and lying down when I reached the top. When I peeked over I could see our camp and the road that traversed it. The road meandered through the pines like a pinky-yellow snake. There were two houses that I could see. The bottom house, which was the first one you'd pass via the road, was a freshly painted white weatherboard bungalow with a blue galvanised-iron roof. The scrub had been cleared for quite a distance around it. A rather dilapidated timber house was closer to where I was lying, with some ramshackle outbuildings adjacent to it along with the remains of what appeared to have been an old slab hut. There were windmills at both houses, suggesting there wasn't a big supply of underground water. Cattle grazed across the cleared country, though I doubted these would be stolen. Instead they'd be used as decoys in case of police visits, while they kept any stolen stock back behind the ridge.

I backed down the ridge and re-entered the scrub on the far side of the old house, proceeding very slowly and carefully now that I was getting closer to what I assumed to be the Challis house. Fortunately, a light breeze was blowing in my face which would be an advantage if the Challises had any dogs. Slipping through the trees, I crouched down when I reached a spot that gave me a good view of the backyard of the house.

My heart thumped when, on using my binoculars, I saw three

men standing about a naked and rake-thin Caroline Clemenger. She was alive, which was a relief, but she was clearly not being well treated. She had a kind of manacle and chain attached to her left leg. The end of the chain was being held by Jack Challis while a hose was being directed at her by what looked like old man Challis.

I snapped some photos and retreated into the trees, but kept my eye on what was going on. After a few minutes, Ted Challis threw a towel at Caroline, who was hunched over with cold. She dried herself while the three men kept watch. Then one of the men threw her a dress which she put on quickly. Old man Challis then unclipped the short chain and escorted her to a small timber hut where, from what I could see, a longer chain was attached to the manacle on her leg. I slithered out of the trees briefly and took some shots before the door was closed. I'd located Caroline Clemenger and she was most definitely alive. I determined then and there to rescue her as quickly as possible.

After a while I crept back towards the cover of trees. I didn't relax my vigilance as I retraced my route through the timber, careful to keep the trunks of the biggest pines between me and the house. It wasn't beyond the bounds of possibility that someone, maybe even Brewster or Reid, could be on the far end of the ridge keeping an eye on our campsite.

When I drew closer to our camp I walked out in a big loop and crossed the creek a couple of hundred metres below it. If there was anything amiss I wanted plenty of elbow room to deal with it.

'Everything okay?' I asked as I approached the hide, where Gaye was keeping lookout.

She nodded and, seeing my expression, asked me if I'd seen any sign of Caroline.

'She's up there, Gaye. Tied up on a chain like a dog,' I said, then told her what I'd seen and that I had the evidence on film.

She looked sombre and said, 'That's terrible but at least we now know she's alive. Congratulations, Lachie.'

'Thanks, Gaye. I better go and speak with Morris.'

I walked up to a place I'd found had better mobile reception and made the call. Morris answered almost immediately and I told him I'd located Caroline Clemenger at the Challis farmhouse and that she was being kept on a long chain like a dog. After we'd talked for nearly twenty minutes about the best way to proceed, we agreed it'd be best if we moved on the Challises in the morning. He said as soon as he got off the phone he'd get his team – including extra police from around the sub-district – organised and that they'd be at the Gorge before daybreak. I warned him that he and his men would need to remain completely hidden in the scrub until they heard from either Gaye or me.

When I returned to camp I debriefed at length with Gaye about what I'd agreed with Ming and then she and I talked about how we'd go about things.

'How do you propose to free Caroline without alerting Brewster and Company? If there's any shooting they'll be straight on to us. Do you think there'll be any shooting?' Gaye asked.

'Not if I can help it. And Morris and his team will be here waiting to raid Brewster's place so they won't be able to intervene at the Challis place. They can do that quite legitimately now that we've located Caroline. Her presence knocks Brewster and Reid for six. Up to today we didn't have a solid case against them, only suspicion. They left no fingerprints and used stolen cars.'

After we'd discussed more of the logistics, Gaye got some gear and set up in the hide. The plan was for her to do the first watch tonight.

Before I went to bed I removed the roll of film I'd used to photograph Caroline Clemenger and the sleazy threesome responsible for guarding her, then put it in a small plastic bag and taped it to my vehicle's chassis. That film, together with Caroline Clemenger's testimony would be enough to put the Challis trio away for quite a long stretch.

CHAPTER 19

I hardly got any sleep that night, so well before 2 a.m. I got up and headed over to take over from Gaye in the hide. She said there'd been no sign of any movement as yet, except from the koalas in the scribbly gum tree. At 6 a.m. Ted Challis drove down into the reserve in a silver-blue Mazda with a bloke in the front passenger seat and someone in the back seat. After pulling up, Challis got out and stood beside the car while the other two men walked across to us. I reckoned from the sketchy description that Sheila Cameron had given me that the more solid, square-built fellow was Brewster so the smaller guy was probably Reid.

Brewster was dressed flashily in maroon slacks and a pink shirt with a dark red tie. Reid was wearing a grey open-neck shirt and dark green slacks. While Brewster dressed like a con man and was undoubtedly a crim, Reid raised the hairs on the back of my neck. He had a mean look about him and I'd had to deal with too many like him not to recognise his type. Adrenaline coursed through my body as I got ready to deal with them.

'Jim Brewster,' the bigger man said and put out his hand. 'And this is a mate of mine, Zane Reid.'

'Laurie Rivers,' I said. 'And this is my partner, Gaye,' I added, gesturing towards Gaye. I shook hands with Reid reluctantly. His hand felt like the scales of a snake and I wondered whether a spell of hard labour in an American gaol had contributed to the texture.

'How's the photography going? My neighbour Ted Challis told me you were looking for black cockatoos. You should try the Castlereagh River. I saw black cockies there last time I was fishing down that way,' said Brewster casually.

'I've got a few nice bird pics but we'll probably pull out later on. I'm going to try for a few more koala shots before we leave. There're a couple of koalas in one of those scribbly gums. You fellows are about early,' I said.

'We're going to the races,' said Brewster.

'Are they on locally?' I asked.

'No, Dubbo,' said Brewster.

'Good punting. I never have much luck with the gee gees,' I said.

'There's good money to be made if you know what you're doing,' said Brewster. 'Sir Crispin is a good thing going in the fourth at Dubbo.'

We talked a bit more, though Jack Reid remained silent. My heart thumped all the while, but they didn't stop long and when they took off I gave them a desultory wave.

'Don't get up, Gaye,' I whispered. 'Go on drinking your tea and talking to me,' I said.

Gaye went one better than that. She got up, settled herself on my lap, put one arm around my neck and rested her face against mine. Her nearness caused my heart to race. I managed to move my head fractionally so that, from the corner of an eye, I could see what was going on. And what was going on was that Reid was watching us from behind a big pine tree.

Reid observed us for perhaps a couple of minutes and then I heard the Mazda start up again and watched it disappear into the dark tunnel of pines. 'The police would have a job catching that baby,' I said. 'It's very light for its horsepower and if Ted Challis can drive at all, he'd leave the police for dead.'

Gaye got off and I quickly moved to a place further up the ridge and rang Morris to tell him that Brewster, Reid and Ted Challis had just left our camp saying they were headed for Dubbo races. I asked him to tell his men to let them go but to stay in position for half an hour to make sure they didn't double back. I couldn't risk Brewster phoning the Challis crew before we arrived. The Dubbo D's could pick up and arrest Brewster and Co by which time I hoped to have Caroline Cleminger in our hands. Above and beyond everything else was my desire to recover Caroline as quickly and cleanly as possible.

'You're letting them go through?' Gaye asked.

'We want to be sure of them, Gaye. If Morris and his men can find evidence at Brewster's place and if Caroline can confirm that they did the bank heist, we've got them on ice and the Dubbo D's will pick them up. Besides, I don't want any chance of a slip-up at the crossroads, not with Ted Challis driving that Mazda,' I said.

I was hugely relieved that the odds against us seemed to have been markedly reduced. I had envisaged a delicate timing operation with Morris and his team masking the Brewster house while Gaye and I tackled the Challis crew.

'Okay, let's get down to business. It would be good if you take the shotgun and a dozen shells just to be on the safe side. I'll take the rifle.'

'Which way will we go?' asked Gaye.

'We'll go the way I went yesterday,' I said. 'There's really no alternative. They'd spot us quick smart if we went up by the road and have Caroline out of there and into the scrub in the blink of an eye,' I said.

I hung my 'Gone photographing' on the bull bar of the four-wheel drive and then we left.

Gaye was very athletic and moved very easily and in no time at all we were at the edge of the ridge. We moved on carefully to where I'd hidden to take the pictures of Caroline Clemenger and the three Challis men. I gestured to Gaye to lie down so we could check what was going on.

I pointed through the trees to where Caroline Clemenger was sitting. She still had a manacle on her left ankle to which a long chain was bolted. I couldn't see the other end of the chain with my binoculars so it was difficult to see how much liberty she was allowed. Close by there was an old shed and through the open door there was a low bed. A little distance beyond there was a door-less latrine.

I whispered that I'd go in by the front door because that was the quickest escape to the cream ute parked below the house, and that she should head in via the back door. If she saw anyone in front of her she should fire one shot into the ceiling to discourage him from taking her on. 'If that doesn't pull him up, fire the second shot at the floor in front of him and then pull out your Browning,' I said.

She nodded, clearly tense.

'You okay?' I whispered.

'Yep,' she whispered back.

'Good, let's get going then,' I said and ran out from the cover of the pines towards the house with Gaye running for the back door.

When Caroline Clemenger looked up, startled, I put my fingers to my lips and she nodded.

Slowing down, I crept around to the front of the house and listened at the front door which, fortuitously, was open. There were voices from inside the house and it sounded as if a card game was in progress. It was time to make a move. Entering the house, I snuck towards the room where the voices were coming from.

Two shocked faces looked up at me as I appeared in the doorway with the Browning in my right hand and the Mannlicher over my shoulder. Jack Challis got up and made to leave by the far door but before he could there was a thunderous blast and bits of ceiling blew around the room. Jack pulled up dead when he saw Gaye standing with the shotgun levelled at him. Old man Challis sat at the table looking shifty. Just then I heard the creak of a floorboard from another room. Next thing the door opened a little and the tip of a rifle barrel poked through.

'Get down, Gaye,' I roared as I launched myself at the door, hurling its occupant back in the process. As the person, a woman, fell backwards, her rifle discharged and I felt a sudden burning sensation at the top of my right shoulder. Gritting my teeth against the pain I saw the woman coming at me with the rifle pushed in front of her. I smacked her hard on the face but she kept coming so I kicked her on the side of her left knee and she fell away from me.

Leaning down, I twisted an arm behind her back and then lifted her and pushed her ahead of me back into the next room where Gaye was positioned in front of the rifle and shotgun in a rack on the wall covering the two Challis men. 'Cuff her, Gaye,' I said.

'Oh, Christ, you've been shot,' said Gaye when she saw the blood running down my arm.

'Don't worry, it'll keep for the moment,' I said.

I went over and checked the two men for weapons but they were clean. Then I checked the firearms on the wall rack behind Gaye, which were loaded. I unloaded them and put the ammo in my trouser pocket.

'Where are the keys of Ms Clemenger's chain, Jack?' I asked harshly.

He didn't answer, just grinned at me, so I picked him up by the scruff of his grubby shirt and threw him against the wall. 'Listen carefully, you creep. I'll ask you just once more, where are the keys to the lady's chain?'

'Hanging beside the back door,' he said, rubbing his hand against the back of his head.

'Can you cuff them please, Gaye,' I asked.

Once Gaye had cuffed them all we tied them together and then to a fence post.

'Are you alright, Caroline?' I asked before explaining that we'd cuffed the people inside and I was going to unlock the manacle.

She nodded but seemed too overcome to speak.

'Were you abducted during the course of a robbery at the ANC bank in Sydney?'

She nodded again.

'Was this robbery carried out by Jim Brewster, Zane Reid and Ted Challis?'

Another nod.

'And have you been held against your will from that time until now?'

'Yes,' she managed in a strangled voice.

'Were you raped by any of these creeps or by Brewster or Reid?' I asked.

'No, only beaten,' she said, her voice hoarse.

'Righto, they're all yours, Gaye. Read them their rights and make the arrests.'

I unlocked the manacle and left it lying on the grass. The police would want to photograph everything. Caroline Clemenger stood up, still crying. 'Thank you,' she said through her tears. 'I'd started to think I'd never get out of here alive.'

'Police reinforcements will be down here in a minute. Do you want to go inside and rest until they get here?' I asked.

'I never want to go in there again if it can be helped,' she replied.

'I can completely understand that,' I said. Just let me go in and get you a comfortable chair and I'll go over and see if my offsider, Gaye, needs any help.

Gaye had finished reading the crooks their rights by the time I got back to them. 'You're in a whole heap of trouble. Holding a person illegally is a serious charge,' I said harshly. 'And you,' I said, looking at the hard-faced blonde woman who'd fired a shot at me, 'You'll probably be facing a charge of attempted murder.'

'Anyone down at Brewster's place?' I asked old man Challis.

'Nah,' he answered in a quavery voice.

'Why not?'

'They've gone to the races,' he said.

'Are you going to let me look at your shoulder?' Gaye asked.

'The medic can do that. Right now there are some very anxious people waiting to hear from us,' I said. 'I'll see if I can raise Morris.'

I couldn't get through to Morris and Gaye's mobile couldn't raise him either. It must have had something to do with the ridge.

I found the keys to the ute and ran it down to the Brewster house which was locked. Spying an axe in the woodheap behind the house, I smashed in the back door.

Inside, I rang Morris and told him that we had Caroline Clemenger and three of the Challis family, old man Challis, Jack Challis and his sister and asked him if he would bring a medic with police up to the Challis place. We discussed organising a counsellor to come out for Caroline straight away but decided it would probably be best to have a medic look at her first and see what he or she thought about the idea of a counsellor. I told Morris I'd been hit in the shoulder and I'd need the medic too.

'I've got to ring Mrs Kendall and Ballinger now so let's talk later,' I said.

'Well done, Lachie,' said Morris.

Congratulations, no matter how low key, coming from someone of Morris's calibre meant a lot to me and I felt quite emotional after I hung up.

I dialled Mrs Kendall's mobile number and she answered

2222222

immediately. 'We've just recovered Caroline, Mrs Kendall, and she's okay,' I said.

'Oh, that's such wonderful news,' she said her voice suffused with relief. 'Thank you so so much. How is she? Can I speak to her?'

'She seems relatively okay physically – though she's bound to be a bit traumatised. We haven't had much of a chance to talk and I've had to travel a couple of ks to get to a landline because of the terrible reception where we are. A medic is on his way to see how she's faring and then she'll be taken to Coonabarabran Hospital for a thorough check up. Once we're back in a place where there's mobile coverage, I'll have her call you straight away.'

'Thanks again for calling me so promptly. I'll never be able to thank you enough. As soon as I get off the phone I'll make arrangements with our pilot to fly up there. We're cleared for night flying so we'll probably leave early a.m.'

After we'd talked about timing and logistics, I rang Police Headquarters, got through to Sophie Walters and told her to tell Ballinger that we'd recovered Caroline Clemenger about half an hour earlier and that the Dubbo police had been told to arrest Brewster and Co who were on their way there for the races.

By the time I got back to the Challis place a virtual flotilla of police vehicles were there and more were coming up the road followed by an ambulance. I told the male medic/ambo that my shoulder could wait while he and his female partner checked out Caroline. Gaye debriefed with Morris, telling him what had happened. The medics finished with Caroline and said she was thin but otherwise in fair shape physically but they'd like her to be supervised overnight in hospital. They then inspected my shoulder. The bullet had ploughed a furrow right on the tip of my right shoulder.

Caroline was very uptight. She hadn't been too weepy with Gaye and me but she went to pieces a bit when the police contingent arrived and she realised she really was safe. There was a policewoman with the team and it took her a while to calm Caroline. She had fits of sobbing and shook like a tree in a gale. After the police had finished a preliminary questioning of her I went over and told her that her mother had employed me to find her and I'd just spoken with her mother from Brewster's house to tell her she'd been recovered. She was at a board meeting but would be flying up to Coonabarabran early next morning.

Caroline said that while she'd always been confident her mother would do everything humanly possible to find her, she hadn't expected it would take so long and lately she'd started to fear she'd never see her mother again. She said it had become very trying to keep up the facade of having lost her memory and that the Challis men, and the woman with them, were a bunch of lowlifes who had humiliated her at every opportunity.

With Gaye ensconced in discussions with her colleagues and the police finished with me for the moment, I asked Morris if it would be okay with him for me to start packing up my camp at the Gorge, 'I don't want to be here when the media arrive. I want the police and Gaye to get all the credit for Caroline's recovery. Keep me right out of it, Ming,' I said.

Morris said that was okay by him and he asked one of the cops to drive me back to the Gorge. The forensics guys arrived as we were leaving and I expected things would remain hectic for the rest of the day with police vehicles tearing up and down the road.

Back at the Gorge, I pulled down the hide and loaded it and everything else bar my table and chairs. A couple of hours later Morris arrived and shook hands with me. 'Congratulations, Lachie. You and Gaye did a truly exceptional job and it's a great result. I wasn't sure you'd be able to pull it off but you did and there'll be a lot of grateful people.' he said. 'Miss Clemenger has gone to pieces a bit. She's so relieved to be able to act normally again she can hardly take in her new situation. Then again she's had to stand up to a fair bit of questioning. Still, she's a gutsy young woman and once she's back home she'll have every facility to get her back to full strength. We feel confident we've got enough evidence to charge them with the ANC bank robbery. Caroline's testimony certainly places them there. We've found a fair bit of money at Brewster's place but it could be race winnings so Miss Clemenger's evidence is all important,' Morris said.

'Have you got her away yet?' I asked.

'Just about to. Gaye and the policewoman are going to go with her and we've got her booked into the hospital,' Morris said.

'Her mother is flying up early a.m. She's got her own plane,' I told him. 'Mrs Kendall is a very important lady in the business world. She's moved heaven and earth to have her daughter found. There wouldn't be many women who would see the Commissioner twice to get advice on how to proceed. I've got a tonne of respect for her,' I said.

'How's the shoulder feel?' he asked.

'The local is just starting to wear off. They gave me some tablets for the pain. It's not too bad. Nothing like last time,' I said.

'Pity that had to happen. Everything else went off so well,' said Morris.

'Gaye deserves a commendation. When I saw the tip of that rifle barrel poking through a crack in the doorway I yelled to her to get down and she still kept the other two covered with the shotgun as well as staying in front of their firearms. She was very cool under pressure,' I said.

'You both deserve a commendation, Lachie,' said Morris.

'Nah, keep my name out of it. I couldn't have done the job without police help right down the line. Also I'm being well paid for my services. It should make good headlines for the cops,' I said.

'As soon as we've apprehended Brewster and the others, I reckon we'll have something on the news tonight. I'd say it would be the main item,' he said. 'I'd better get back and see what's happening,' said Morris.

'Yeah, I'm sure she'll get through it,' I said.

What will *you* do now, Lachie?' said Morris.

'I'm going to finish packing up here and head back to town. I'll stay with my sister tonight and look in at the hospital to see Caroline tomorrow morning,' I said.

'Do me a favour and don't say anything to Gaye about me pulling out. Just tell her I thought she did a great job and that I couldn't have had a better partner. Tell her I didn't want to be around when the media hawks arrive because I want the focus to be on her and you guys,' I said.

'If that's the way you want it,' he said.

'That's the way I want it. I take it that your boys or the Stock Squad looked for stolen cattle on the Challis place?' I said, changing the subject away from Gaye because I'd grown close to her and it was going to be hard to leave her.

Morris nodded. 'More than once.'

I told him about the creek paddock back in the pines and how to find the place. 'There are cattle there now and maybe they're stolen cattle. You might be able to nail the Challis bunch with some additional charges.'

'Thanks a lot for that, Lachie,' Morris said with a gleam in his eye. 'We've been after that old bugger and his family of cronies for years.'

'It's a clever set-up. They've drilled a tunnel through the end of the ridge and camouflaged two gates. I wouldn't have known about it except that I went that way to look for Caroline,' I said.

Morris walked back to his car. 'You'll come and see me before you leave?'

'Of course and I'll be watching the news tonight,' I said, smiling.

'Okay, see you, and thanks again for everything you've done,' he said before driving away up the hill.

I looked around the campsite. Even though my job was done I had the strangest feeling about leaving this place. Though I'd been here for only a couple of days I'd experienced real happiness with Gaye. There was a strength and dignity about her that touched me deeply. I'd also appreciated her willingness to share in the duties about the camp. There was no rancour about her and she certainly wasn't self-centred. Besides her personal qualities I felt a huge sexual attraction towards her that I hadn't experienced for many years. I had the strangest feeling that despite the difference in our ages, we could make a real go of marriage. But I was determined that, no matter what, I wanted to marry a woman who was keen to live on a farm.

I had just about finished packing everything in to the four-wheel drive when a police car skidded to a halt on the sandy track beside the campsite and the two-striper who I'd met on my way to Coonabarabran wound down his window. The one-striper beside him was the young chap who had talked photography with me.

'G'day, Mr Photographer,' the two-striper said with a grin. 'You're a turn-up for the books. You did a great job.'

'Thanks,' I said.

'I was right when I said I'd seen you before,' the two-striper said. 'You were in a picture with the Sergeant and a couple of other blokes who got medals,' he said, giving me a grin and a thumbs-up before taking off in a cloud of pink dust.

I took a last look at the rock pool and waterfall and then I got in my vehicle and drove away.

CHAPTER 20

I thought a lot about Gaye as I drove back to Coonabarabran before forcing myself to concentrate on my future plans.

I intended to return to Sydney and hunt up some temporary accommodation while I worked out what to do next. I cursed my brother for being such a dickhead. I didn't blame Nicole one little bit for leaving him and putting his future ownership of Kamilaroi on the line. He'd got himself involved with another woman and Nicole wasn't the kind of woman to wear that.

It would all be a great concern for Mum, who didn't deserve to be worried at her time of life. She hadn't experienced an ideal marriage but there had been compensations because she'd loved us children and then got on well with Nicole. And she loved Stuart and Nicole's three girls. She wouldn't be enthralled with the prospect of another woman taking Nicole's place and I didn't blame her.

The possibility of Kamilaroi going out of the family saddened me enormously because when it all boiled down I loved the place. It was a big property, running excellent sheep and cattle as well

as producing good crops most years. It wasn't the greatest grazing or cropping country but there was a uniqueness about it that
tugged at my heart. The smell of rain on the distinctive sandy-pink
soil and the delight I experienced in mustering sheep and cattle in
pine-dotted paddocks were just a couple of reasons I loved it. But I
couldn't work with Stuart. It was as simple as that.

I would have to find another property somewhere else. I'd had a
gutful of dealing with crims and crime. I wanted to work on the land
again and be part of a community of decent, hard-working people
who talked sheep, cattle and crops. I wanted to get married again to
someone who shared my love of the land. And I wanted two or three
kids to grow up with the same appreciation for the country I had.

As secrecy no longer mattered, I detoured to buy a carton of
beer and a couple of bottles of white wine. After that I dropped
into Tiger Murphy's butcher shop to buy some meat.

'Lachie Sinclair!' Tiger boomed when he saw me walking into
the shop. We shook hands enthusiastically – we'd played cricket
together and he'd been there when I'd heard the terrible news
about Kenneth.

'How're things, Tiger?' I asked.

'Fair enough, Lachie. Still keeping my head above water. The
cockies are still whingeing and still buying flash cars. There are a
lot more tourists coming here now that the local mob have done
something about Coona's history. What brings you back to the
bush?'

'I had a case here. You might see it on the TV news tonight and
I suppose the local rag will blow it up. It was a joint operation with
local and Sydney police,' I told him.

'I heard rumours about a big operation out at the Brewsters. Jeff Ashcroft – he's a new ambo – dropped in and said he was headed out to the Gorge,' he said.

Lord, but news travelled fast in the bush. You couldn't spit but the entire population would know about it inside the day.

Flora was surprised to see me back so soon but, as always, pleased too. 'I expected you to be away for at least a week,' she said as she kissed me.

'We managed to wrap up the case fairly quickly,' I said as I handed over the drinks and meat.

'I told you that we don't expect you to bring anything, Lachie. We don't see much of you and we love to have you with us,' she said.

'I like to contribute, Flora. How are your guests?' I asked,

'Still a bit apprehensive. At least Nicole is. Vickie is getting a bit restive. She isn't a girl who likes to be tied down. What on earth happened out there?' Flora asked.

'Watch the evening news tonight, sister dear. There's a big story about to break except that I won't be mentioned in it. The police will get all the credit but that's the way I want it. I'm being well paid for what I did so they're welcome to the limelight,' I told her.

'Have you thought any more about Kamilaroi?' she asked.

'Fairly constantly, Flora. I don't like the idea of parting with my third of it but I can't see any way around it. Yes, I could come back to my third of the place but I don't want to be feuding with Stuart for the rest of my days. In ordinary circumstances Stuart might be able to buy me out but he's going to lose half of his third of Kamilaroi if the divorce goes ahead so he won't have the equity to borrow money to buy me out. He might be able to borrow enough to pay Nicole her half of the settlement. What are you planning to do with your third of the place?' I asked.

'Laurie and I discussed it in the light of the anticipated divorce. We'll probably hang on to my third. We don't need the money and we're putting what it makes into a fund to pay for the kids to go to university. We could probably pay Stuart some sort of a manager's wage to look after the place. It might help him through a difficult period,' Flora said.

'That's very generous of you and Laurie. He's acted like a little Hitler since he took over the running of the place, given that he's done a good job. Still, nobody can stand him. Tiger Murphy told me he doesn't buy Kamilaroi livestock now because he's got no time for Stuart. I never thought he'd stoop to whacking Nicole. And I believe he slapped Vickie too,' I said.

'Yes, he did,' agreed Flora.

'Flora, as much as I hate the idea of breaking up Kamilaroi, I think it's time for me to pull up stakes and start off somewhere else. I'll talk things over with Mum tomorrow,' I said.

'Is there a woman on the horizon for you?' she asked.

'Only in my dreams, but I'm at the stage now that I'd marry again if I could find the right person,' I said. 'And she'd want to live on a property because I'm determined to go back to the bush.'

'Have a shower and a drink, Lachie. You look a bit worse for wear,' said Flora.

'Thanks, Sis. I'm all right,' I said, though the thought of never seeing Gaye again still had me feeling despondent. 'I have to make a call to Sydney before I do anything.'

I sat down in Laurie's office and rang Mrs Kendall and gave her a more comprehensive report than I'd had time for earlier in the day. The important thing was that she had her daughter back. She'd lost a bit of weight and she probably still had a few bruises from the beatings the Challis lot had given her but otherwise she was healthy enough. How she was mentally was another matter. I told Mrs K that Caroline had been transported to Coonabarabran Hospital and that I would call and see her in the morning. I assured her that Caroline hadn't been raped.

Mrs Kendall said she hoped she'd see me at the hospital. 'Thank you again,' she said warmly. 'I don't understand how you managed it but that doesn't matter right now. I've rung the Commissioner and given him my thanks and congratulations. I realise it was you who broke the case but I also recognise that the police went right outside their usual role to support you and I'm really most grateful that they did,' she said.

She was, of course, right. I couldn't have pulled it off without police support. Having Gaye with me, not to mention the way she played her role, put the icing on the cake.

Next I rang Christine and gave her the news that we'd successfully resolved the case and that Caroline Clemenger was safe and being checked over in hospital. She was thrilled, of course. I told her I'd be back in a couple of days and we talked for a little while about what had been happening in Sydney while I was away. She and Dasher clearly had everything under control. I told her that my sister-in-law and my niece might arrive before I did and perhaps she'd be able to help get them settled into the Neutral Bay place.

After a shower and a drink I felt a whole lot better. Nicole was very restrained but Vickie was very bubbly. Sheila was a bit brighter on this occasion and looked nice in a red pant suit.

Needless to say everyone sat in utter silence when the television news came on. Caroline Clemenger's rescue and the arrest of local man, Jim Brewster, and his associate Zane Reid, along with several members of the Challis family, dominated the news. Gaye stood with Senior Sergeant Morris and his area superintendent while he was being interviewed. It was a huge success for the police.

There was a babble of conversation in the aftermath and Vickie asked me if this was the case I'd been involved in. I told her that it was but that I didn't want to talk about it.

When the front door bell rang unexpectedly all conversation ceased. Nobody else was expected for dinner.

When Flora came back from answering the door Gaye was behind her and my heart leapt.

'There's a young woman here to see you, Lachie,' said Flora with a glint in her eye.

'I hope I'm not interrupting your dinner,' said Gaye looking just a mite less assured than I remembered her out at the camp. Perhaps she hadn't expected so many people.

Before I could reply, Laurie, in true Laurie fashion, leapt to his feet. 'You're not interrupting dinner. We haven't started yet. Please stay and have dinner with us. It's just a family gathering. Here, let me get you a drink. What will you have?' he asked.

Gaye looked at the drinks on the table before answering. 'I'll have a white wine, thank you.'

Laurie grabbed a chair and put it down next to mine before handing her a glass of wine.

'Have you had dinner?' Flora asked.

'No, I haven't long finished at the station. There was some stuff to wrap up and I'm going out bush again in the morning,' Gaye said. 'Are you sure I'm not interrupting anything?'

'Of course I'm sure,' Flora said with one of her million dollar smiles.

Gaye sat down and leaned over towards me. 'You didn't give me a chance to say goodbye to you,' she whispered.

'Sorry about that. I hate goodbyes. And I didn't want any nosey parker reporter finding me there. I wanted you and the police to get all the credit,' I said.

'Well I wasn't too happy to find you gone. I thought we were on a better footing than that. Giving me and the police all the credit for a job of that dimension is one thing but running out on your partner without saying goodbye is something else,' said Gaye.

'You were busy and I wanted out of there. The job was done and it was all police work from there on,' I said.

'I'm . . .'

But whatever Gaye was about to say was interrupted by Brett.

'We just saw you on television. You're a detective,' he said.

'That's right. I'm a detective,' Gaye said with a smile.

'Do you have a gun?' Brett asked.

'Yes, I do,' said Gaye.

'Crikey,' Brett stammered.

Back in the dining room I found Vickie in conversation with Gaye. They had their heads together and seemed to be getting on very well. Maybe Gaye would be a good contact for her in Sydney. I couldn't imagine my niece coming to any harm in Gaye's company.

I reckoned it wouldn't be long before Flora got Gaye away under some pretext so that she could winkle more out of her than she'd managed with me. Sure enough, supper gave her that opportunity.

After all the family had gone to bed, Gaye and I were left alone in the dining room.

'Lachie, why did you clear off so quickly?' Gaye asked.

'My job was done. I didn't want to be there when the media gang arrived. I wanted to give you and the police the opportunity to shine. I couldn't have done it without yours and their support. It will do the police in the area a lot of good. Besides, I hate good-byes,' I said.

'But we worked so closely together on the case,' she said.

'Look, I enjoyed working with you, Gaye. You're a talented cop and a very nice person to boot and I have some good things to remember from our stay out there. The assignment wouldn't have been the same without you,' I said. 'Are you going back to Sydney tomorrow?'

'No, probably the day after. I have to go out to the Challis place and Morris wants me to show him that cattle set-up you located. I think Morris has been in touch with the Stock Squad about it,' said Gaye.

'I see. Well I'm sure you'll get a commendation and a promotion. I'll be telling Ballinger that you came up trumps,' I said.

'Thank you, Lachie. I want you to know that I think you're the best person I ever worked with,' she said.

'Thanks,' I said. 'This will probably be my last case unless there's more waiting for me in Sydney. I've decided to get out of this game as soon as I can manage it. I hope you go a long way. You'll be a sergeant in no time after this.'

'Maybe, maybe not. I haven't decided that I'll stay on for the long term. I'd like to get back to the bush too. If my Dad had been a better manager I'd have a place to go back to today but the "ifs" make a lot of difference, don't they?' she said.

'An awful lot,' I agreed.

I saw her to the door and then walked with her out to her car, heart racing. I wanted more than anything to put my arms around her but was too scared of rejection to do so. I reckoned that maybe heaven was very close but the thought of being wrong held me back.

'I'm going to sell out my share of Kamilaroi and buy a property somewhere else. We'll draft the sheep and cattle three ways and I'll have more than enough to stock a decent property. Finding that property will be my major priority,' I said.

'Half your luck,' she said, looking at me for a while before opening the car door. 'Take care, Lachie,' she said, and kissed me on the cheek.

'You too, Gaye,' I said.

'I'd certainly like to know where you find that property,' she said, pulling a slip of paper from her bag and writing on it. 'That's my mobile number if you'd care to let me know.'

I stood and watched her car pull away feeling a real sense of sadness. Heaven had just turned the corner and I'd allowed it to happen.

CHAPTER 21

Next morning when I sat down for breakfast, Flora took up from where she'd left off the previous morning.

'You could have let on that you liked her,' she said out of the blue.

'Liked who?' I asked.

'Don't be obtuse, Lachie. Gaye Walker, of course,' she said.

'Who wouldn't like her? Gaye is a great person. Look at how the kids took to her straight off,' I said.

'Gaye is interested in you, Lachie,' said Flora.

'Drop it Flora,' I said tersely. 'I'm going up to the hospital to look in on Caroline Clemenger, after which I'm going to call and pay my respects to Senior Sergeant Morris, after which I'm going to head out to Mum's.'

'It'd be good if you told Mum you're thinking of marrying again and moving back to the bush somewhere. It would really cheer her up. She'd love more grandchildren and it would get her out of that big old house now and again,' Flora said.

I pointed out that thinking of marrying again and actually having someone to marry were two quite different things but I supposed it wouldn't do any harm to tell her I was hoping to meet someone special. I left it at that because it was very difficult to win an argument with Flora, who would have made a good police prosecutor. Instead I set off for the hospital.

'Caroline's been asking if you were coming,' the charge sister said after I arrived and introduced myself. 'Come along,' she added, heading down the corridor.

Caroline looked much better, though she was still prone to being teary. 'I didn't get a chance to thank you properly yesterday. It was all so hectic and I just felt in a daze. Gaye was lovely. She said it was you who worked out who was holding me and where I might be. I'll never be able to thank you enough,' she said.

'You did very well to hold out there for as long as you did. It was extremely courageous of you,' I said.

'Gaye said you completely hoodwinked Brewster and Reid by pretending to be a wildlife photographer,' said Caroline.

'I didn't really have to pretend much because wildlife photography is my hobby,' I said. 'And you can thank your mother for being so persistent. If it hadn't been for her and her efforts you might never have been found. I don't think I've ever heard a woman as relieved and as happy as when I rang to tell her we'd rescued you. I'm a big fan of your mother,' I said.

'She's great, isn't she? But I still don't know how you managed to locate me,' said Caroline.

'A little bit of information, some following up of hunches and a lot of luck,' I said.

'I don't think any luck was involved. You managed what nobody else was able to do,' she said.

'The police deserve a lot of credit. They bent the rules to back me from go to whoa. Your mother talking to the Police Commissioner helped but they didn't have to back me up and they did. It was all pretty irregular and it was lucky I'd worked as a policeman and helped them after I left the force, otherwise they wouldn't have considered doing all they did for me – even with your mum's influence.

It was inspired of you to come up with the amnesia act. Not many young women could have pulled that off. Was it a snap decision?' I asked.

'Actually, it was,' she said, smiling.

'It may have saved your life. But I'll talk to you more when you're back in Sydney because you've had enough stress for now. What matters is that you're safe. Brewster, Reid and the Challis bunch are in custody and I reckon they'll be locked up for a long time,' I said.

'Thank you again for all that you did,' she said, putting her hand on my arm as I got up to leave. 'Would you allow me to take you to dinner when I've recuperated in Sydney for a while?'

'Sure,' I said with a smile.

'I'll want to know just how you found me,' she said.

There was a knock on the door before I could say anything more and we both looked up to see Mrs Kendall, who ran over to the bed and took Caroline in her arms. They hugged each other for several minutes and there were tears on both of their faces, making it a very touching reunion and one that I've never been able to forget. I pushed a chair up for Mrs K as she got off the bed.

'I would have been here earlier except that I went to see Senior Sergeant Morris to thank him for his help,' Mrs Kendall told me and Caroline.

It was a mark of the class of the woman that she'd gone to see Morris before she even came to the hospital to see her daughter. She was some woman.

'You must have had a very early start, Mrs Kendall,' I said.

'I wanted to get here before the media pack arrives. Senior Sergeant Morris was full of praise for you, Mr Sinclair. He outlined how you managed Caroline's rescue. You and that young policewoman. You're a remarkable man, Mr Sinclair,' she said.

'Thank you, Mrs Kendall. I've just finished telling Caroline what a great mother you are. It was your persistence and determination to appeal to the top echelons of the police force that made the difference. Now you'll want to talk to Caroline by herself and I need to go and see my poor neglected mother before I head back to Sydney,' I said.

'When I get back to Sydney I'll be calling you,' said Mrs Kendall. 'We have some business to conclude. I hope the vehicle was satisfactory.'

'It went like a bird,' I said.

'Then it's all yours,' she said before putting her arms around me and kissing my cheek. 'Thank you again. From the moment I met you I felt as if a great weight had been lifted from me.'

'No worries. Good luck with the media and keep my name out of it if you can. Give all the credit to the police here and in Sydney and to Gaye,' I said before turning to leave. Restoring Caroline to her mother was probably the most satisfying bit of detective work I'd ever done.

My next call was to Coonabarabran Police Station to say goodbye to Morris. 'Everything tied up?' I asked after I'd been ushered into his office.

'There are still a few loose ends but it's a very good outcome, Lachie. We're yet to take a full statement from Miss Clemenger but we'll leave that until later today. We found two big stashes of money at the Brewster place and a smaller amount at the Challis place. There could well be more and we're still looking. Mind you, Brewster could have hidden money where we'll never find it. Brewster and Reid deny they were involved in either bank robbery and claim that all the money we found came from their punting. Miss Clemenger's evidence will be sure to blow that claim away. We haven't let on that she was shamming loss of memory so they're not aware that we can definitely tie them to the first bank job. We'll hit them with that when we oppose bail,' said Morris.

'Did you do anything about the creek paddock?' I asked.

'Constable Walker is out there with one of my blokes and a fellow from the Stock Squad,' said Morris.

'Excellent. I'll be interested to know if you find any stolen cattle,' I said.

'I'll let you know,' said Morris. 'How was Miss Clemenger this morning?'

'She looks one hundred per cent better than yesterday. She'd had her first hot bath in some weeks and her mother has brought up clothes and makeup for her. She wants to take me to dinner when she's feeling better. How about that?' I asked.

'I'd take her up on that offer, and go for oysters and lobster that night,' said Morris, laughing.

'I might just do that. Do you need me any longer?' I asked.

'No, feel free to leave whenever you want to. You can write a report and give it to Ballinger when you get back to Sydney and he can send me a copy,' he said.

'Okay. I'm going out to spend a night at my mother's in case you need me,' I said. 'Thanks again for your help. I realised from the outset that I was placing you in a difficult position but the results have justified the means, thank God,' I said.

'We came out of it extremely well and head office couldn't be more pleased, Lachie,' said Morris.

I could understand that. The police force was under constant pressure to perform and looked bad when they were unable to apprehend the perpetrators of big-time crime. They always liked it when they made quick and successful arrests.

'That's good,' I said. 'If you come down to Sydney before I leave there maybe we could do a spot of fishing together. I've got a boat. That is, Luke Stirling and I have got a boat.'

'I suppose you've got plenty of gear,' said Morris.

'I sure have . . . heaps,' I answered, smiling. 'I don't know where I'll end up or if there'll be any fish wherever that might be but I'll let you know.'

'So you're definitely going back to the land?' said Morris.

'I definitely am but there's going to be a lot of messing about before that happens. It will take time to sell up my third of Kamilaroi and then to find a suitable property. I'll probably have to arrange a bridging loan if I find a decent place,' I explained.

'Sounds as if you're going to be very busy,' Morris said.

'Very, but I'm looking forward to it. I've got a clear objective and that makes a difference,' I said.

'Well, if it happens that I don't see you for a while, the very best of luck. I feel fortunate to have worked with you. There's not many people the force would back like they backed you, Lachie,' Morris said.

'Don't I know it. I hope they treat you right. I better hit the road, Ming,' I said as we shook hands.

I felt pretty good as I drove away from the police station. I couldn't have asked for a better way to finish up in the crime business. I'd been trusted to the hilt by the police and I'd repaid their trust.

CHAPTER 22

I had mixed feelings as I drove out to see Mum. I expected her to be sad about me severing connections with Kamilaroi but in the final analysis I had to do what was best for my future.

Contrary to my expectations, Mum was philosophical about my decision. 'That's fine, Lachie. I understand you wanting to buy your own property. I hope you find what you want and then perhaps you'll get married and have some children. That would make me very happy,' she said.

'When I do manage to buy a place, you'd be very welcome to come and live with me,' I said.

'Thank you, but no, this is my home. No matter what happens with Stuart's divorce settlement, I'd like to stay here while I'm still healthy. I've always loved this place and I love it even more now that I'm independent. I'll get a few acres surveyed and put into a different title. Flora and the kids are nice and close and most of my friends live in the district. I'll come and visit you but I won't live with you,' she said.

I knew her reference to enjoying it more now she was independent referred to not having to put up with my father. I reckoned it was the dead right time to ask her what I'd wanted to ask her for years but had always shied away from doing.

'Why did you marry him, Mum? Did you ever love him?' I asked, half expecting her to tell me it was none of my business. Perhaps, strictly speaking, it wasn't but I wasn't a naïve little boy who accepted his parents for what they were. I was used to asking questions and getting answers and I regarded my mother as a very special person. I hadn't always behaved in exemplary fashion where she was concerned but that didn't alter the fact that I loved her.

She looked at me and nodded. 'I've been wondering how long it would be before you asked me that.'

'You can tell me to mind my own business but then I'll always wonder,' I said.

'Upper-class girls were expected to marry and have children when I was younger. They weren't expected to go out and earn a living. I wasn't trained for anything other than how to run a home. Why did I marry your father? No, I never loved him. He was a fine looking man from a good family and Kamilaroi was a noted property. There wasn't anyone with as much to offer,' she said.

'But you . . .' I stammered.

'How did I feel about sleeping with him? My mother told me that it was something every girl had to do and you just had to put up with it. It was a necessary part of married life because that was how children were conceived. I thought that sleeping with your father would be less unpleasant than sleeping with any of the other prospective husbands in my circle of friends. So I married him and he gave me four children and all of you gave me a lot of pleasure. I was heartbroken after we lost Kenneth, and Stuart has always worried me because he has the weakest principles of you all. But Stuart is a fine manager and a tireless worker. And he is my son and that's all there is to it. Are you happy now?' she asked.

'I had it pretty well worked out and what you've told me more or less confirms it. I couldn't see that you ever loved Dad or, for that matter, that he loved you. But you ran the homestead well and, best of all, you were a great mum. Those early years before I went away to school would have been very hard if you hadn't been here. But I still wonder how you were able to put up with Dad for so long. You and Dad were like chalk and cheese,' I said.

'Perhaps we were but we had fairly clear lines of responsibility. I ran the house and he ran the property. The only times those lines became blurred was where you children were concerned. I thought he was too strict on you. He'd commanded soldiers and was very strong on discipline, often too strong. Yes, I think he contributed to Kenneth's death but for the sake of the family I couldn't come out and say what I really thought. I would have had to leave your father and it would have split the family. I needed to be there if only to be a moderating influence where Stuart was concerned. Now he's gone and got himself involved with another woman and is going to have a hard time affording to buy Nicole out, he's going to have to come down off his high horse and be just another grazier,' she said.

'But even if he gives Nicole half of what he owns Stuart will still be relatively well off,' I said.

'Granted. And don't forget that Flora pays him a wage for

looking after her share of Kamilaroi. No, he won't be badly off but he won't be a kingpin grazier like your father was,' she said.

'Maybe that will tone down his highhanded behaviour,' I suggested.

Mum steered away from talking any more about Stuart, focusing on her concerns for Nicole and Vickie instead. She pressed me to keep her up to date with their progress in Sydney, and I promised I would.

After lunch Mum and I sat down in the lounge room to discuss the likely course of events from a financial viewpoint if, as now seemed likely, Nicole divorced Stuart and he married another woman.

Up until Father willed me a third of Kamilaroi, Stuart and Flora had provided Mum with a modest income and they paid all her electricity, fuel and other costs. Stuart provided two thirds and Flora one third. After I was willed one third of the property and its livestock I'd kicked in one third. Mum didn't really need our money as she had money of her own and what we gave her was more in the nature of a tax dodge: better that Mum had it than pay it away in taxation.

'You needn't worry about me,' said Mum. 'I've done well with the investments I've made with my own money and I could get by quite well without any support. I'm more concerned about you, Lachie. You need a wife, a proper wife, and I'd like a couple more grandchildren. Is there any woman on the horizon for you?' she asked.

'I'd say more over the horizon than on it,' I replied. 'I'd really like to get out of Sydney now and I'd like to marry someone who'll want to live on a property. Seeing the kids up here has confirmed how much I want to have children, too. But I'm going to be extremely busy for a while. Apart from looking out for Nicole and Vickie, I've got my agency to sell while I work out with Stuart what portion of Kamilaroi I can get surveyed so that I can offer it for sale. Apart from all that I want to find a property both to live on and graze my share of Kamilaroi's livestock on. If I find a decent property I'll probably have to get a bridging loan to tide me over until I can put my share of Kamilaroi on the market,' I said.

'You must let me know if you find the property you want. I could loan you the money until you sell your share of Kamilaroi,' she said.

'It would run to a lot of money, Mum,' I said.

'That's all right. Both Dad and your uncle Ben left me quite a lot of money and all I've ever really spent was what I put into this house. And Laurie's made some excellent investments for me over the years. I can't see that I'll have any need of it so you may as well use it. Better than paying interest on a bridging loan,' she said, smiling.

'You're a wonder, Mum,' I said.

'Ideally, I'd prefer to see you back here and I know that you would too and if you could resolve your differences with Stuart you'd make me very happy. But I'm a realist so I know that's unlikely. If the divorce proceeds and Stuart brings a new woman here that won't help matters either. So, as much as I'd like you back here I think the best thing you can do is buy your property and live the kind of life that makes you happy. Flora rang and told me that there's a policewoman she thinks is quite keen on you. Is she the one over the horizon?' she asked.

'Maybe she is and maybe she isn't. She's a fair bit younger than me and she's got a big future in the police force if she wants it. Her uncle is a bigwig in the force. He used to be my boss. Gaye comes off the land and she's pretty keen on the bush and very keen on horses. She's a great girl and we got on very well but that was for only a couple of days during a dangerous assignment. How we'd get on long-term is another matter. That said, I think you'd like Gaye,' I said.

'Well, we'll just have to wait and see, won't we? Let matters take their course,' she said.

'I don't propose to make the same mistakes I made with Fiona,' I assured her.

'That's encouraging,' she said with a gleam in her eyes. 'I would very much like to meet Gaye.'

'If you meet her I'll be very much farther down the track with her than I am today. But right now I've got an awful lot to do,' I said.

I had laid out my position as honestly as I was able and I could do no more. There wasn't much I wouldn't do for Mum but I wouldn't put up with Stuart. I had to make an attempt to tolerate him because I'd have to deal with him about the subdivision of my third of Kamilaroi and with the drafting off of one third of the property's livestock. But while the subdivision was relatively urgent, the division of sheep and cattle wouldn't happen until I had a place to put them.

The rest of the day was largely spent in the kitchen where Mum ran up two tins of her incomparable shortbread for me to take back to Sydney before she turned in earnest to preparing dinner. The steak she cooked was from one of our steers and literally melted in the mouth. Together with baked potatoes, onions and spinach, and topped by Mum's glorious gravy, it was a meal I remembered for days. It was followed by fruit salad and cream and ice cream.

'That's the best meal I've eaten for a long time and I've been to a few good restaurants in Sydney,' I said. 'That was a meal and a half.'

'I hope your young lady over the horizon is interested in cooking,' she said.

'In the short time I was with her, she told me she liked cooking, which Fiona never did. Her idea of a meal was to find some new restaurant where they only gave you enough to fit in the corner of an eye. I used to be hungry a lot in those days,' I said.

It was great to have Mum to myself. She'd known heartbreak and loss and she'd put up with an autocratic husband for most of her life. She had suffered through my divorce and now she was going to have to endure the breakup of her eldest son's marriage. Yet despite all this, my mother was a grand lady and I'd never heard a bad word said about her. I hoped there was some way I could make her really happy. I loved her and I was proud of her.

CHAPTER 23

I dawdled over breakfast and didn't get away from Kamilaroi till mid-morning. It was tough to leave Mum even though Stuart wasn't far away. I'd always loved her but I'd never been able to talk about the things that really mattered. This time we had and I felt all the better for it.

On the way back to Sydney I decided to camp in the wine country on the southern side of Merriwa where I bought some wine for Christine. I also poked about and took some pictures of birds. I was lucky enough to get a couple of pics of a curiously mismarked magpie that was more white than black.

Next morning I made an early start and, on reaching the outskirts of Sydney, drove first to my house at Neutral Bay. After stacking all my new camping gear way in the toolshed I sat and had a cuppa with Nicole and Vickie. They'd only arrived late the previous afternoon but they already looked much happier than when I'd last seen them and were very pleased with my house and its location.

I arrived at my office just before midday where I found Christine drinking coffee while talking on the phone to Dasher.

'What's doing?' I asked when she got off the phone.

'Greetings, Oh Great One. I hear you covered yourself in glory and are now universally popular with everyone in the Force,' she said before handing me a couple of faxes and some printed-out emails from quite a number that were on her desk. I scanned them quickly and handed them back to her. 'Okay, so that's that. What else? Oh, by the way, thanks for helping Nicole and Vickie to get settled in yesterday,' I said.

'No worries at all. They're both lovely. There's nothing of immediate concern happening. Probably about a couple of hours of going through paperwork to get it up to date,' she said.

'Hmm. Where's Dasher?' I asked.

'Having the day off and awaiting your commands, Oh Great One. Actually he was commanded to mow the lawns which he hadn't done while he was in here with me. He'll be in tomorrow morning,' said Christine.

'Poor henpecked old bloke. Have you heard from Luke?' I asked.

'Twice, actually. He rang yesterday evening and said that you-know-who was very pleased with you,' she said. 'And so he should be. You did all the nutting out and took all the risks – including getting shot again – to rescue Caroline Clemenger. And you also managed to identify the bank robbers and let the police get *all* the credit. Why wouldn't they be pleased?'

As it turned out we worked well into the early evening. Christine took me through a couple of reports Dasher had done and updated me on some new potential clients and their requirements.

All of this would look good for a person looking to buy my agency.

'Thanks for that,' I said when we finally called it a day. 'Let's head out to dinner.'

'Sure. By the way, what was she like?' she asked.

Who?' I asked.

'Gaye Walker. Who else?' she said. 'A little bird told me that DSC Walker is a real bombshell.'

'I thought you might have meant Caroline Clemenger. Well, DCS Walker is a very capable woman who did her job very well,' I said refusing to rise to the bait. 'She'll probably get a commendation and get pushed up to sergeant very quickly.'

'That reminds me, apropos of your accommodation dilemma. Somebody's already offered you accommodation now that Nicole and Vickie have taken over your house,' she said.

'Really?' I said with some astonishment. 'But how could anyone have known?'

'It seems that Mrs Kendall found out somehow and her cousin Rosemary happens to own a very large house with oodles of rooms to spare and would love to have someone "really trustworthy" come and stay there. And who more trustworthy could she have but the lovely man who rescued dear Eunice's daughter,' she said. 'That's the address and that's the phone number. I know you're being very self-sacrificing giving up your house for Nicole but you can't camp here indefinitely. It's only a stopgap measure.'

I looked at her and shook my head. She was always sorting things out without taking any credit and finding me accommodation was just the latest in a long line of things she'd done for me and others over the years. I was going to miss having Christine around. As well as loving to help people she was very entertaining with a sure-fire sense of humour and a very sharp business brain.

'Chris, if I sell this agency and somebody buys it as a going concern, would you want to stay here?' I asked.

'But why would you want to sell it given how well this last case has gone? You'll have cases galore after this,' she said.

'I'm sick of dealing with crims and I've decided to pull the plug. Going up to Coonabarabran confirmed to me that I'm a country boy at heart. I'm going to sell my third share of Kamilaroi and that ought to give me enough to buy a decent property. I'll get a third share of the sheep and cattle from Kamilaroi so I'll be able to stock any farm I buy with top quality stuff straight away. Then there's Mrs Kendall's money which might come in handy for something. Finding the right property will be my major priority over the next little while so I'm not interested in new cases. As of this moment the agency is on the market,' I said.

'I see. Well, I guess any decision I make would depend on who bought it. If it was Dasher or some other retired cop I might be persuaded to stay on. It's a very congenial place to work,' she said.

'I'd have to get Paul's agreement for the agency to remain here. He might want to charge market rent for someone else. He's been very fair with me. Mind you, I've put a good number of investors his way,' I said.

'That you have,' she agreed and then picked up two pieces of paper and handed them across to me. 'By the way, Cousin Charlie sent this to me.'

Cousin Charlie was one of Christine's affluent relatives but more to the point he was a financial guru who made a large percentage of his income dealing in shares. He had a soft spot for Christine and was continually tipping her off about what shares to buy and sell. Christine had passed this information on to me several times and I'd done very well out of it.

I whistled through my teeth as I digested Cousin Charlie's latest financial advice. 'What are you going to do about it?' I asked.

'I'm going to follow his advice,' she said.

'Do you want to put some of your Kendall money into these shares?' she asked.

'Maybe. Would you mind making me a copy?' I asked.

'You can keep that. It is a copy,' she said.

'I've appreciated you passing on Cousin Charlie's tips, Christine,' I said.

'I know that,' she replied.

'I've made enough money from those tips to buy me the best Hereford bull in Australia. If I get him I'm going to call him Charlie,' I said.

'You could hardly call him Christine,' she said.

'That's what I'll call his first heifer calf,' I said.

'Moo,' she said in a very fair imitation of a calf calling its mother. I shook my head. I was definitely going to miss Christine.

After dinner with Christine I slept at the office and woke feeling very bright. I had a scratch breakfast of toast and vegemite and two cups of tea before I headed off to see Rosemary Mitchell about living with her while I tried to sell the agency and find a good property. I drew up outside a large grand home with a great view of the harbour. According to Christine it had been in Rosemary's late husband's family for yonks and was worth a pretty penny.

Rosemary turned out to be an extraordinary woman who'd lived a highly adventurous life. She'd climbed in the Himalayas, sailed extensively in the south Pacific and, wonder of wonders, photographed orchids in the Amazon jungle. Her late husband, who'd been her companion for most of her forays, had died from something he'd picked up in New Guinea and she told me she'd been thinking for some time of taking in a boarder both because she liked company but also because she needed money to augment her income. I later learned that it was Rosemary's 'adventures' that had inspired Caroline Clemenger's travels across the planet. Rosemary had taken Caroline on her first such adventure to an African game park followed by a hike up Mount Kilimanjaro.

A few days after I moved in with Rosemary, I received word that DS Ballinger wanted to see me.

'You got my report, Super?' I asked after we greeted each other.

'Yes, and this job you did was probably the best bit of "police" work by an individual I've seen in my career in the Force. The Commissioner agrees with me. He wants me to take you up to see him if that's okay with you,' Ballinger said.

'It's very generous of you to say so, though I had a lot of luck,' I said. 'And of course, I'd feel honoured to see the Commissioner, especially as I'm not a serving member of the Force.'

'Ah, yes, well, we'll talk about that later. And I don't think luck had a lot to do with your success. Yes, you were probably fortunate Brewster and the other two cleared out to go to the races, but I don't doubt that you would have got Miss Clemenger away and then it would have been up to the Coonabarabran police to nail Brewster, Reid and Challis. Yours was an extremely well thought-out and executed operation. You took a punt on them being in the Pilliga because of Ted Challis coming from there and your friend spotting Caroline Clemenger, and it paid off. Posing as a wildlife photographer was a very clever idea to allow you to get close without causing suspicion. Likewise, Gaye Walker was the icing on the cake, so to speak. You were right in what you told Senior Sergeant Morris. It was a get-in-quick and get-out-quick operation.'

'I couldn't have done it without your backing, Super. At the outset Morris was understandably sceptical and concerned about the irregularity of it. He nearly had a fit when I broached the subject of going in to the Pilliga with a young policewoman. But DC Walker came up trumps,' I said.

'Well, we can't give you another gong, you not being in the Force, but I understand that you're being recompensed handsomely for your efforts,' Ballinger said.

'That's true,' I admitted.

'There's one interesting development you wouldn't know about. We've not long had word back from the FBI regarding Zane Reid. We sent his fingerprints across to them. The FBI said Reid has a record in the US and skipped the country ahead of a murder charge. He came here either illegally or with a false passport. They want him back and they're welcome to him,' he said, before being interrupted by the trill of his office phone.' After speaking to someone briefly he hung up and said, 'I'll take you up to see the Commissioner now.'

The Commissioner welcomed me warmly before gesturing for Ballinger and me to sit down.

'I'd like to personally thank you for the job you did, Lachie. It was a massive result. I'd also like to say that, speaking for the New South Wales Police Force, I am most appreciative of you unselfishly giving the credit for the success of the operation to the police. The media would have made a hero of you,' he said.

'Thank you very much, Commissioner. I couldn't have done the job without your backing and you took a risk punting on me. If anything had happened to DC Walker the fat would have been well and truly in the fire. I'm going to be paid well for my efforts and I'm very happy for the police to get all the credit. I'm very chuffed that you were prepared to back me, an ex-cop,' I said.

The Commissioner nodded and cleared his throat. 'DS Ballinger and I have been wondering how you'd feel about coming back into the Force, actually. Though you'd have to return to your old rank initially, I could guarantee you an inspectorship fairly quickly. You could go right to the top, Lachie. We could backdate your re-enlistment and say you were working undercover with DC Walker,' he said.

It was a fairly staggering offer and it floored me for a few moments, but my mind was made up about my future. 'I'm flattered that you think enough of me to make such an offer,' I said. 'But I'm sorry, I can't accept.'

'You prefer what you're doing to police work with all the protection it offers?' the Commissioner asked.

'Yes and no, but that's not what it's about anymore because as of today my agency is on the market. I've made the decision to leave the crime business and return to the bush. I've decided to sell my third of Kamilaroi and use the proceeds to buy a property. But don't imagine that I'm unaware of the significance of your offer,' I said.

'The land is getting tougher, Lachie,' said the Commissioner, taking off his glasses and subjecting me to one of his legendary appraisals. 'I've got relatives on the land who tell me that these days you need a good big place to make a go of it.'

'There are still plenty of viable properties, Commissioner. It depends a lot on the kind of place you buy and how capable you are at working it. I won't be battling as my third share Kamilaroi represents a fair whack of money and I'm also getting a third of the stock on it. Anyway, it's the lifestyle I want more than how much I can make from a place. The bush is where I was born and it's where I feel most at home,' I said.

'Ah, well, I'm disappointed because you'd have had a good future here but if the land is what you want, I hope you do well,' said the Commissioner, taking my decision with good grace.

Afterwards Ballinger walked me back to his office and we had a bit of a chat. As I made to go he wished me the very best of luck and thanked me again.

'Super, come fishing with Luke and me sometime before I clear out for the bush,' I replied.

'I'll take you up on that, Lachie. I mean it,' said Ballinger. 'By the way I hear that you and DC Walker got on well.'

'DC Walker is a great young woman and a first class detective. She was very cool when the Challis woman was threatening us with a rifle. I enjoyed my time with her. In fact, it's lucky the op finished when it did because I was starting to feel too strongly about her. She likes the bush too,' I said.

'Like that, eh?' he said.

CHAPTER 24

A fortnight passed before Mrs Kendall made an appointment to come and see me. I'd told Christine not to worry about billing her for the time being. Mrs Kendall had paid me for four weeks in advance as well as generously giving me the four-wheel drive and I'd ended up only working for about a week so it seemed somehow wrong to accept the $250,000 she'd offered to pay me for rescuing Caroline.

Meanwhile, I'd been focusing on helping Nicole and Vickie get settled in at Neutral Bay.

Christine brought Mrs Kendall into my office on the dot of the time we'd arranged.

'Mrs Kendall, how nice to see you again and looking so much happier than the first time we met,' I said, getting up.

'Thank you. I'm very happy and Caroline is getting better and cheerier with each passing day. She's sleeping much more soundly now and hasn't cried for a few days,' she said before sitting down.

'That's great news,' I said.

'It's a bit too early to say she'll fully recover. She had a couple of panic attacks when she first ventured out to the shops but she seems better now,' she said.

'Well, she did go through quite an ordeal,' I said.

'Why haven't you sent me an account, Mr Sinclair?' said Mrs Kendall, never one to beat around the bush.

'To be honest, I didn't feel comfortable sending you an account. You paid me for four weeks' work and I was involved for only one, not to mention you giving me a top-of-the-range four-wheel drive vehicle and some very nice camping gear. It just doesn't feel right to ask you for the full amount you offered, especially since you were so worried at the time,' I said.

'Nonsense! You put your own safety on the line to save my daughter's life and I can never really express my gratitude fully. You were shot and you could have been killed. A deal is a deal, Mr Sinclair. You don't owe me anything and I owe you what I offered you and that's all there is to it. Besides, Rosemary told me you're thinking of buying a property and I'd love to think I can help you,' she said.

With that, she used my desk to write out a cheque for $250,000, which she passed across to me.

'Thank you,' was all I could say. It was by far the most money I'd ever held in my hands.

'Not at all. Having my daughter back safe and sound is worth more than any amount of money. How do you like being with Rosemary?' she asked.

'It's great. Rosemary's a very nice woman and we get along well. Thanks for arranging that, Mrs Kendall,' I said.

'It was no trouble at all,' she said. 'Now, I'd really like you to come around for dinner with me and Caroline. When would be a good time?' she asked, her invitation sounding more like a Royal Command. No ifs, buts or maybes.

'Whenever suits you, Mrs Kendall,' I said without hesitation.

'Very well, then Caroline can pick you up from Rosemary's this coming Saturday evening at six o'clock,' she said.

Caroline did pick me up very close to six – clearly she shared her mother's attitude to time. When she got out of her car to greet me, I hardly recognised her as the woman I'd rescued. Wearing a beautiful blue dress, she was groomed to perfection and had put on some of the weight she'd lost over the two months she'd been held. Despite what Mrs Kendall had said about her state of mind, she looked both happy and tanned.

It turned out that Mrs Kendall was unwell, so we ended up going to a restaurant on the water at The Spit. Caroline was clearly well known there and was greeted effusively before we were escorted to a table a little distance away from the others with a great view of the water.

As we ate our entrée Caroline and I talked about how she'd been bearing up. She told me she'd slept poorly the first week back in Sydney and that she was still on sleeping pills and had nightmares but had started to feel a lot better over the last couple of days.

Caroline told me that the abduction and subsequent incarceration had shaken her. Although she had met people of many nationalities, this had been her first experience of what might be termed the lower strata of men and their morality.

I tried to steer her away from the subject of her abduction and on to other areas. She had a very good general knowledge and was very widely travelled so a lot of what she told me was quite fascinating. And despite her privileged background she was very down to earth and direct.

When I asked her what she was planning to do next she said she was thinking of spending a couple of months on the Barrier Reef to try and fully recover her confidence, which had been battered by her abduction and being held prisoner. As she told me this tears sprang to her eyes and she said she wanted me to know how grateful she was that I'd found and rescued her.

'As I said, you should really try to forget about all of that,' I said. 'I know the police have your statement so there's no need to go over it again with me.' Unlike Caroline, I had had a great deal of experience with thuggish men and their morality, women too, and now I wanted to put the thought of them behind me. But Caroline didn't let up.

'You were so clever working out where I was that I feel you should know the full story just in case I never see you again. If you hadn't found me they might have killed me. I heard Reid saying that they should 'get rid of me'. But Brewster said he wanted to find out who I was and see if he could get some money for me. The Challis men used to taunt me about Reid. They said I knew too much about all of them.'

The words flowed out of her like something she had to be rid of so she could take up her life again.

'There were about a dozen of us in the bank at the time the robbers appeared. The main man grabbed hold of me and pulled me to the door of the bank. I banged my head badly on the door and must have blacked out. When I came to I was in a car with the two men I came to know as Brewster and Reid. I didn't show any sign I'd regained consciousness and was careful to only open my eyes when their voices indicated they were turned in the opposite direction. All I could gather was that we were in a private car park and they were waiting for someone called Ted.

'I was extremely frightened but I realised I needed to keep my smarts about me to outwit them. That was when I made the snap decision to fake a loss of memory.

'When Ted Challis came back with the other vehicle, we left the underground car park and headed out of Sydney. We drove well into the night until we finally arrived at Brewster's farm. They kept me there for a few days and I told them I couldn't remember my name or where I was from except that I lived in a big house with two storeys. I used to sing snatches of opera and musical comedy which amused Brewster but not Reid. At first I don't think they believed I'd lost my memory. However, with time my behaviour seemed to convince them. I had a big lump near one eye where my head had hit the bank door and it went down to a black and yellow bruise so that probably helped me to convince them that I'd lost my memory.

'Brewster and Reid used to go to races all over the place so I was a nuisance to them and they paid the Challis crew to look after me. Brewster kept telling them he thought I was worth "big bikkies" and they'd better not let anything happen to me.

'On my first day at the Challis place, old man Challis told me to take off my good clothes and all my "fancy underwear" and when I refused they manhandled me and took off my clothes. Because of my defiance they held me over a work bench and Jack Challis and the old man belted me with lengths of polythene pipe. When they'd finished they told me that if I didn't do as I was told they would give me a hiding every time. Then the old man gave me a piece of yellow soap and turned a hose on me. They gave me that old grey dress I was wearing when you rescued me and put a manacle on one ankle and padlocked it to a long chain. They'd unlock the padlock if they wanted me to do the cooking and washing.'

'There's one point I'd like to clear up,' I said, interrupting her. 'Why did they take you into Coonabarabran, Caroline?' I asked.

'It was really because of Reid. He wanted to kill me and bury me in the scrub. The Challis lot were really frightened of him. One day when the Challis boys cleared out for some reason – probably to steal stock – Brewster was guarding me and he gashed his leg badly chopping wood. It was bleeding a lot and Brewster got very panicky about it and said he'd have to go to town so it could be stitched. He didn't trust Reid enough to leave me with him so he insisted on taking me with him. Reid sat next to me the whole time and said if I moved six inches he'd shoot me. He had a silencer on his pistol so he might have.

'So I sat in the car with him while Brewster went in to the surgery to get his leg stitched. When Sheila Cameron came outside and looked at me I was pretty sure she'd recognised me so I turned my head away and hummed songs like I was a bit of a ninny. But by this time I think they were convinced that I really had lost my memory,' said Caroline.

'Brewster was the best of the bunch. I'm not saying he was any good, because he wasn't, but he had a bit more to him than the

223

others. Reid was pure poison. He said I was a witness to what they'd done and that could only mean trouble for them. The Challis lot were a bunch of low life creeps. They got a big thrill out of humiliating me and making me do what they wanted. They used to call me the "rich bitch". "Get the rich bitch down here to cook dinner," they'd say, and "Get the rich bitch to do some washing." That sort of thing. And they always stood around gawking when the old man hosed me down with cold water.'

'That's terrible,' I said. 'It's amazing you've recovered as well as you have.'

'They were a sick lot. Occasionally Reid would come and talk to me to try to work out if I'd really lost my memory. It was hard keeping up the pretence. I knew Mum would be doing everything in her power to find me and that kept me going. But I didn't think it would take so long. You've got no idea the relief I felt when I saw you and Gaye run past me. I knew that everything was going to be all right,' she said.

I patted her on the arm as she dabbed at her eyes with a tissue. 'You're safe now. They're all in custody and I reckon they'll all be locked away for long stretches. You've come through your ordeal very well. Many a person would have gone to pieces completely in your situation. For what it's worth I think you were very brave and very clever to play that memory loss stunt and maintain it for so long. Not many people would have thought to do that and it probably saved your life. You've got a lot of backbone, Caroline. The Barrier Reef sounds just the place for a nice long break,' I said.

'I'm enjoying being back in a familiar environment though,' she said. 'Home seemed very far away when I was chained up with the

Challis crew. I used to cry whenever I thought about either home or my mother. It was my belief in her that kept me going,' said Caroline.

'Your mother is a remarkable woman,' I said 'and so are you and Rosemary.'

'You need a younger Rosemary, Lachie,' she said.

'Don't I know it,' I said.

'Not to worry. Something tells me that your luck might be about to change,' she said.

CHAPTER 25

About a fortnight after my dinner with Caroline, I received a phone message from Mrs Kendall asking me if I could call around the next morning to visit her and Caroline. I'd told Caroline that I was selling the agency then going bush to look for a property, so I assumed I was being summonsed for a final thank-you and farewell.

Mrs Kendall lived in an imposing two-storey mansion in Rose Bay with a truly magnificent garden, including an extensive lawn which was in good enough shape to host a bowls tournament.

Mother and daughter were, as usual, beautifully dressed.

We chatted about some of the recent developments we'd heard about. I told them that Zane Reid had turned out to have a record as long as your arm in the US and the FBI had applied for his deportation back to America.

After a very pleasant morning tea, Caroline walked with me to long red gravelled drive where I'd left my car. 'I hope you find the kind of property you want and the wife to go with it,' she said and gave me a hug and kissed me. 'And I hope we can keep in touch?'

'We'll have the trials to endure and I suppose I'll be called as a witness,' I said.

'I'm trying not to think about the trial,' she said.

'That's the stuff. And if ever you come to visit me I hope we can go riding together,' I said.

One Friday morning in the weeks that followed I rang Judy Stirling and asked if she and Luke and the kids would like to spend Sunday up at Wagstaff. She said that Luke had had a couple of tough weeks and could do with a break so they'd love to join me there.

I'd been very busy myself so I was also looking forward to a day up at Wagstaff. After spreading the word about the agency being for sale, it looked like I had a buyer. Ballinger had sent an ex-detective called Dick Pollard to see me. Dick been invalided out of the Police Force after being injured in a bad car accident – though except for a slight limp, he appeared in fair shape. Christine thought he seemed too 'gentlemanly' to be a detective but he'd worked in housebreaking with some top cops so I was confident he'd know his way about.

I'd also travelled up to Kamilaroi to have my third of the property surveyed, though not without several acrimonious exchanges with my brother. He wanted the best of everything which included most of the major improvements such as the woolshed, yards, silos and the two homes – mother's and his – though he was fine to let Mum use the main house for the rest of her life. I wasn't prepared for either Flora or me to get a bad deal so we surveyed up what would be Flora's portion. Both Flora and I got more land than Stuart to make up for the improvements on his block.

We also ended up getting Stuart to agree to hive off five acres surrounding the old homestead and give them to Mum with her own separate title. All of this was costly and involved a lot of work but we had no option. I hadn't put my block on the market because I was giving Stuart time to investigate whether he could raise the money to buy it. I doubted it would be possible because he had to find a lot of money to pay Nicole half of everything he owned, but he was my brother so I had to cut him a bit of slack and gave him two months to organise finance, after which time I proposed to advertise my block. In the meantime I started looking at properties for sale.

The Stirlings and I set off early for Wagstaff and got there before 8 a.m. We put the boat in the water and then fished up and down the channel for an hour or so. I fished for luderick with green weed and Luke opted for a hand line with pieces of mullet for bait. The luderick here were real ocean-going fish showing more bronze than usual. I caught three good sized fish and Luke landed a big flathead.

After a while we moved up to Half Tide Rocks and put Judy and the kids ashore. A middle-aged couple were fishing from a small open launch kellocked to the left of the rocky point. We left all the gear for lunch and pushed out for open water. There wasn't much chop as there was only a very faint breeze. But there was always some degree of swell when you got away from the shore. It was winter but it was a clear day and warm enough in the sun not to have to wear a heavy jacket.

We fished on for a while and it was sheer bliss to be out there on the water with my best mate. We didn't have to talk, just being together was sufficient. Presently, with the slap of the ocean against the side of the boat and the gulls screaming as they dived for tiny fish, I asked Luke as casually as possible whether he'd heard anything of Gaye Walker.

'Apparently she's resigned, Lachie,' he said. 'The Super told me that Mrs Kendall gave her a new car and a decent amount of money for her part in helping you find Caroline Clemenger.'

'But why would she resign?' I asked, stunned. 'She had a great future ahead of her in the Force.'

'Seems funny to me, too. Funny peculiar, I mean,' said Luke, looking at me appraisingly.

I quickly turned the conversation back to other things. I could hardly believe what I'd heard. I hadn't been able to get Gaye out of my mind because I felt sure she was the woman for me. Yes, she was several years younger than me but she had a good head on her shoulders and she liked the bush.

We fished for a while longer and then cruised back to shore where we had the freshest possible flathead for lunch. Was there a nicer fish? Was there a sweeter fish? I doubted it.

Judy reminded me that Luke's birthday was coming up and she hoped I wouldn't be away for it. I asked her how she felt about having the evening meal at my Neutral Bay house. We could have a barbecue under the big Moreton Bay fig and the Stirling family could meet Nicole and her daughters. It would be good for Nicole to meet some new friends as she seemed a bit lonely without the strong social network of friends she'd had in Coonabarabran. I'd probably invite Christine too as she was steadfastly resisting getting involved in any kind of relationship, and I was sure she'd get on with Nicole and Judy. Being the mover and shaker she was, she might be able to use her networks to help get Nicole some work.

'That's a lovely idea, Lachie,' said Judy warmly.

'Okay, we'll do it,' I said. I didn't tell her that I planned to invite Gaye in case she didn't come. I thought having Gaye there with some other friends might allow me to put my toe in the water, so to speak. If I was rebuffed then that would be the end of it but I wanted to glean some idea of whether there was anything between us or not. Thinking about my last contact with Gaye in Coonabarabran I'd begun to wonder if I'd acted badly on that occasion. Now I had to know one way or the other whether there was any chance of a relationship between us, especially before I finalised my choice of possible properties to buy.

I rang Gaye on her mobile and said that if she wasn't busy would she like to come to my place at Neutral Bay for an evening barbecue. 'It's Luke Stirling's birthday and his and Nicole's kids will be there. No dressing up. Very informal.' I got it all out in a rush and waited anxiously for her answer.

'I'd love to,' she said without hesitation.

'That's great,' I said, relieved.

Gaye asked me what I'd been doing and I told her in abridged form that I was on the verge of selling my agency and had done some preliminary property-hunting on the internet.

'What have you been doing, Gaye?' I asked without letting on that I'd heard she'd resigned from the Force.

'Oh, this and that. I resigned from the Force,' she said.

'Why did you do that? You had the world at your feet,' I said.

'Mrs Kendall sought me out when I got back to Sydney and insisted on giving me a decent amount of money and a car and I've been doing a couple of courses,' she said.

'Well, I'm stunned. I thought you'd be well on your way to making sergeant,' I said.

'There are more important priorities than making sergeant – no matter how worthwhile that would be,' she said.

I wondered what those priorities were and hoped she'd elaborate when we spoke at the barbecue. Gaye had intimated when we were at the Gorge that she wasn't in the police force for the long haul. However to resign so soon after being actively involved in what was regarded as a police triumph seemed a bit odd.

The day and the weather were both on our side for Luke's birthday barbecue. Nicole's three girls all helped out making salads, though when the Stirlings arrived the two younger girls quickly teamed up with Roger and Kate. Vickie clearly regarded herself as too grown-up to be with the younger kids and opted to keep helping Nicole and me get things ready for the evening. Vickie was in the middle of a secretarial course which was only a stopgap measure while she worked out what she really wanted to do. Christine was also coming early to help. She knew Gaye was coming and I suspected she wanted to be there when Gaye arrived because she'd been subtly trying to discover whether I was secretly seeing Gaye and not telling her.

I handed over Luke's birthday present which was a new you-beaut fishing reel.

'This might be called aiding and abetting in the commission of a hobby,' Judy said when she saw it, then laughed. Judy was a great sport and I couldn't imagine her and Luke ever splitting up. The world would blow up before that happened. They were two solid people who took problems and difficult periods in their stride.

There was a momentary break in our preparations when the two female bombshells finally met – one blonde and one brunette. They were both wearing jeans because I'd stressed that this was a very informal gathering.

Christine watched me very closely all through the evening, though I always made it my business to spend time with everyone, including the kids, at these sorts of gatherings. Roger and Kate Stirling rated a close second to Flora's two in my books. I'd been privy to some of their biggest problems and secrets and they regarded me as "okay for an older person".

It was a pretty good barbecue. The steak was first class and there were chops and sausages galore along with the salads. Nobody drank too much and I drank very little because I wanted to finish the evening with my wits intact. I was anxious that Gaye didn't leave early because I wanted to have a serious talk with her.

There was no shop talk between Gaye and I because we couldn't discuss police matters in front of anyone but Luke. Instead, we talked about a lot of things, including horses, farming and properties.

'So you're just about ready to go bush to look for your property?' Judy said.

'I'm heading off this week,' I said. 'I've got a lot of information from various agents. At the moment, most of them are either too large or too small.'

'Where do you fancy looking first?' Judy asked.

'I'll poke about Central Western New South Wales. I know it reasonably well because I had my first police posting there. If I can't find anything suitable I'll need to look elsewhere. I don't want a place with frigid winters or one that's too far from a town and schools. It's too hard on your family, especially kids,' I said.

'You don't have any kids though,' said Christine.

'Well I sure hope to have kids,' I said.

I could have gone on talking about land and properties for most of the night but I didn't want to bore them with that sort of stuff on Luke's birthday. I tried to stay clear of Kamilaroi too because that was a touchy subject for Nicole and the girls.

Everyone pitched in and we washed up in no time and finished up with supper which was Luke's birthday cake washed down with tea or coffee – or soft drinks for the kids. After Luke was given his presents people started to leave.

Finally, only Gaye was left, and we walked out past the Moreton Bay fig and just beyond where the big outside light illuminated part of the back lawn.

'I'm glad you came, Gaye,' I said, thinking it was all or nothing now.

'I was surprised you invited me,' she said.

'Really! Why?' I asked.

'You couldn't get away from the Gorge quickly enough,' she said. 'I took it that you'd had enough of my company. And that night at your sister's place you were almost off-handed.'

'You couldn't be more wrong, Gaye. I was damned scared if I saw any more of you I'd make a fool of myself with you. I didn't know how you felt about me. And I guess, truth be told, I didn't feel up to dealing with being rejected,' I said, realising again what a blind fool I'd been. I should have known that last night in Coonabarabran. I was supposed to be a hotshot detective and I hadn't been able to detect what Gaye felt about me. How dumb could a fellow be?

'There hasn't been a day that I haven't thought about you. But how did you know what I felt about you. I tried not to show it,' I said.

'I knew even before Morris told me what you said that you liked me. I put in my resignation not long after I got back from the Pilliga. I realised you'd been badly affected by your divorce. It was you or the Force,' she said.

I put my arms around her and we kissed.

'We're so silly to have wasted so much time,' said Gaye. 'Why didn't you come straight out and say what you thought? For a smart man you've been very obtuse. Your mother told me she couldn't understand you. Yes, I went to see her. I'm going to get on very well with your mother, Lachie.'

'Mum didn't say you'd been to see her.' I said.

'I asked her to keep mum about it. Literally. Your mum's a grand lady. She told me quite a lot about you, Lachie. I knew I wouldn't get it out of you,' she said.

'I thought you deserved better than me, Gaye. A younger fellow. And some women don't like second-hand blokes,' I said.

'Oh Lachie, you're always putting yourself down because of your failed marriage. These things happen. You were married to a woman who had different values. You're a great person, smart and with lots of integrity. The kids all love you and they're usually very good judges of character,' said Gaye.

'What are these courses you're doing?' I asked, looking to change the subject a little.

'Cooking and first aid. I wanted to improve my cooking and I thought the first aid might come in handy if I went back to the bush,' she said, smiling.

'Hmm,' I murmured.

'Here we are with things finally sorted out and I'm going to have to leave you to look at properties,' I said.

'Yes, but if you find the right property you may never need to leave me again,' she said.

My heart beat faster because Gaye had just answered the question I had been about to ask her. 'No, I won't,' I agreed.

'I'd like to be going with you but I've started these courses and I'd like to finish them. It may take weeks, even months, to find what you're looking for. I'll be here and ready to go when you are,' she said.

'If and when I find a decent property I'll want you to see it before I close the deal,' I said. 'If you don't like the place, I won't buy it.'

'You couldn't be fairer than that, but I'm sure if you like it I'll like it,' Gaye said. 'Mind you, we won't always agree.'

'No, I know. How did Ballinger take your resignation?' I asked.

'Reasonably well. He joked that that's what he got for sending me up to work with you. He told me what you'd said about me so I knew I hadn't misjudged what you felt about me,' Gaye said.

'Well I must say it's a great relief to know where we stand. I can leave to look at properties with a clear mind. I'll let you know how I'm going. Have you got any preference for locality?' I asked.

Gaye shook her head. 'Not really. The most important thing is to have a place that can pay its way. I'll have to leave you to work that out. I don't want a terribly fancy house either. It wouldn't matter if it needed some attention just so long as the property's right,' she said.

What a woman, I thought. So different to Fiona. I'd found a treasure and I didn't want to lose her. We'd got on well at the Pilliga camp and hopefully we always would.

I'm afraid we were very late leaving my house that night but when we left we knew what was in front of us and I think it would be true to say that we were very excited by what the future promised.

CHAPTER 26

Buying a property was a very special undertaking. It meant, for starters, outlaying a lot of money. It also entailed a high degree of judgement. The wisest and most successful landowners bought properties that suited their objectives. Thus a grain grower wouldn't look for a property in New England or anywhere else where it was difficult to grow either winter or summer grains. The major emphasis at Kamilaroi when I was growing up was on sheep and cattle but it was also possible to grow either winter or summer crops there, which in fact we did to a greater extent in the bad years for beef and wool.

What I was looking for was a smaller property similar to Kamilaroi where I could run decent numbers of sheep and cattle while being able to grow some grain – oats, certainly – depending on prices and seasons. If there was scope for some irrigation, so much the better. There was no way I was going to be locked into a property that wouldn't allow me the latitude to diversify. I also wanted a property that was big enough to support an extended family should one of my kids want to stay on the land. Lastly, I wanted a property that was in reasonable proximity to a decent-sized town with adequate medical and educational facilities.

I'd been in touch with several agents in the general Central West of New South Wales because I knew the area better than anywhere else. My first police posting had been in Parkes and I'd driven to most of the towns adjacent to it at one time or another. There were good places in several areas but they just weren't big enough to be viable unless there was enough water for irrigation and in most cases there wasn't. Cowra and Canowindra were attractive areas but they were 'social areas' – by which I mean that they were considered very desirable areas and attracted a premium. City business people who didn't have to rely on farming for their primary income bought properties around these areas. Mudgee was the same and had a lot of winemakers and hobby farmers in the district.

There were some nice wool-growing properties in the general Yass area but some of them could be fire traps with their long summer grass and rocky hills where it wasn't possible to plough firebreaks. You couldn't guard against every possible disaster but I had a particular horror of fire. Likewise country that went under in a flood. River country was valuable if the river stayed within its banks. You could even tolerate some flooding along the river but not a flood that covered most of a property.

I drove a lot of miles and stayed at a lot of pubs and motels but it was turning out to be very difficult to find the kind of property I was looking for. I thought my next step would be to change direction and drive up to the Delungra-Warialda region where I knew there was some good country.

Just by chance I dropped into the Forbes sheep sale where I met a sheep buyer called Greg Hamilton who'd bought sheep from us at Kamilaroi. He was surprised to see me there because he thought I was a cop. I told him I'd left the Force and was selling my portion of Kamilaroi so I was looking for a property and that so far I hadn't found what I was looking for. He asked me what kind of property I was looking for and I summarised what my ideal place would be in a few sentences.

'You could do worse than look at that country west of the Warrumbungles,' he said. 'Some of the best sheep I buy come from that area. I'd recommend basing yourself at Gilgandra and having a dekko north and south of there.'

'Isn't it all light country . . . red, sandy stuff?' I asked.

One of the things my late father had preached was the desirability of a property having both black and red country – that is, heavy and light country. The lighter country comes quicker after rain but goes off quicker and the black country needs more rain but lasts longer.

'There's plenty of that and it's good crop country but there's heavy black self-mulching and red loam soils. They're growing good lucerne too. I reckon it might be some of the best value-for-money country going these days. It grows helluva good stock and there's some good merino studs in the area. It's fairly close to Dubbo too so you've got most of what you want in the way of hospitals and schools there.'

Greg Hamilton knew sheep so I gave a lot of credence to what he had to say. I'd hoped to head back to Sydney to see Gaye that weekend but I decided to put that off for a few days while I scouted the Gilgandra area.

I rang Gaye and gave her my regular update on what I'd been up to and where I'd been to look at places and then told her what Greg had said.

'What do you think, Lachie?' she asked.

'I don't know the area well at all even though it's not much more than an hour or so west of Kamilaroi,' I said.

'Your mother would be pleased if you bought a place there,' she replied.

'I suppose she would but so far I'm not having any luck. Maybe I'm due for a change,' I said, laughing.

'I've got my fingers crossed,' said Gaye. 'I'm missing you, Lachie.'

'I'm missing you too, sweetheart, but the sooner I can find us a place, the sooner we can be together. The property is the first step to everything,'

'The Pilliga was the first step to everything, Lachie,' she said.

Which of course it was only we didn't know it then.

Early the next morning I set off for Gilgandra, which was about forty miles north of Dubbo and right on the Castlereagh River. The region was first explored by John Oxley in 1818. The Castlereagh River, unlike most of the longer rivers of central and western New South Wales, did not have its headwaters in the Great Dividing Range and the average flow wasn't up to some of the other western rivers. In fact it ranged from quite low to flooding. The Castlereagh was sometimes referred to as 'the upside down river' because stretches of the river disappeared underground, leaving only pools, but there was some very good country along the river.

I made contact with a local agent, Hugh Bailey, who was a walking encyclopaedia about the Gilgandra district. For the next two days he took me to properties north, south, east and west of Gilgandra though I didn't see one that I really liked. The price per acre ranged from around $200 to as high as $350 per acre and one property had recently been bought for that price. The people who knew values said it would take that buyer years to make money out of it. The farming country was the dearest.

I asked a few local farmers for their idea of how much country I'd need to make a living but opinion was divided on this. A few said at least 1,500 acres and some said more. I was of the opinion that with costs going up the way they were, you'd need at least 3,000 acres and more for preference but no properties of that size were on the market. They were there – plenty of them west of Gilgandra – but they weren't up for sale.

Hugh Bailey said he was sorry he couldn't show me what I wanted but to keep in touch because properties came on the market from time to time. I'd come to the decision to head back to Sydney and take stock when he said, 'Look, it might be worth you paying Mrs Gordon a visit. She's been making noises about selling out since old Harry died but hasn't got around to actually doing it.'

Hugh went on to tell me that Harry Gordon had finished sowing a paddock of oats, brought the tractor back to the shed and dropped dead as he got off it. 'The old lady has been battling for months. She's got arthritis and can't do much. The neighbour's fifteen-year-old boy planted her latest crop of wheat. He's a terrific kid and helps her a lot in other ways. If you get on the right side of her she might decide to sell,' said Hugh.

'What's the area of her property?' I asked.

'It's roughly 4,000 acres and there's some river country in it. Harry didn't do as much farming as some. He liked sheep and cattle best. The stud cattle you'll have from Kamilaroi would do well on the river country,' said Hugh before pulling out a map and showing me where the Gordon property was to be found.

I thanked him and promised to tell him how I got on.

I drove out after breakfast the next morning and found Mrs Gordon feeding a pen of lovely Rhode Island Red hens. She was leaning heavily on a stick and making heavy weather of the job. I introduced myself and admired her hens and told her that my late father kept very nice Australorps at Kamilaroi.

The old lady looked at me in surprise. 'You're not *that* Lachie Sinclair from Kamilaroi?'

I assured her that I was. 'Fancy that now. I remember you when you were a wee boy. Your lovely mother put on a very nice lunch for me and Harry and we bought a bull from Kamilaroi – and a very good bull he was too.'

She went on to tell me that they'd had Herefords for some years before Harry got bitten by the Angus bug and crossbreeding. I took the bucket of grain from her and after a little while we moved across to the big homestead where she insisted on giving me morning tea.

While she was getting things ready we nattered away and it was clear she'd been very lonely since her husband died. She needed knee operations but wouldn't leave the property to have them. She had no children and her closest relative since Harry's death was a widowed sister in Dubbo.

'Oh, I don't know what to do, Lachie. Harry loved this place but I can't do anything now. Young Johnny Hunter comes over and helps me when he can but he's at school most of the time and I can't rely on always having him.'

I told her that Hugh Bailey had suggested I come and see her just in case she had come to a decision about selling Glengarry.

She considered this for a little while and then said, 'I know I need to think about selling but it'd be such a wrench. That said, I know you'd look after it well so I'd be happy for you to have a look over the place and see what you think.'

I thanked her and said it'd be great to look around and she offered to take me over the whole place if I could do the driving because she'd got to the stage where driving for too long was quite painful. As we toured the property it was clear everything was in good order and the state of the place spoke volumes for the effort Harry Gordon had put into it. There were machinery and hay sheds, grain silos, a three-stand woolshed and good set of cattle yards. The sheep yards needed a bit of attention but they were the only part of the property I could find fault with. But even with the sheep yards there was a covered race which was a big plus when handling sheep.

I was particularly pleased that the fencing was all in good order, with the river country fenced into multiple paddocks to allow maximum use of the richer ground. There was a mix of heavy black ground while farther away from the river the black or grey soil gave way to red loam. The timber was mainly box with some pine on the red country. There was timber in every paddock though the paddocks farthest from the house had the most. There was also an area fenced off for lucerne, which Mrs Gordon assured me could be watered though her husband had found it a bit much for him to handle towards the end of his life.

I tried to estimate the acreage and though it had to be at least 3,500 acres though Mrs Gordon said it was closer to 4,000. It wasn't anything like Kamilaroi in area but it was better country in some ways. After we'd driven back to the homestead I had a longer look at the machinery. There were three tractors – two John Deere's and an old grey Ferguson. I had a soft spot for the 'Fergy' because I'd learned to drive on one of them. There was an oldish header and a variety of machinery including a couple of augers and tanks of petrol and diesel in a separate shed. There was probably enough machinery to handle the acreage of grain Harry had grown. An old set of stables was full of bales of hay.

The house was a four bedroom clad home with enclosed verandahs. It had a large kitchen with both Aga and electric stoves. Both the kitchen and the bathroom had been renovated recently. The lounge and dining rooms were large and there was a good-sized office. It was a comfortable home, not flash, but very liveable.

Over lunch, which Mrs Gordon insisted I stay for, I asked if she'd be prepared to sell it to me?

She said that if she didn't sell it she'd have to put a manager on to run it and go and live with her sister in Dubbo. If she put it on the market she'd have to put up with a lot of people going through the house. Then there'd be all the worry of a dispersal sale and she'd see all Harry had worked for go out the front gate. It would be very distressing.

I knew almost from the first moment I arrived at Glengarry that this was the place for Gaye and me. Three generations of the Gordon family had lived in the homestead and over the years they'd added to the original block. Through good and bad seasons and the iniquitous death duties, the place had given them all a decent living. My Herefords and my sheep would do well here. There were noted merino studs not far away like Weealla at Balladoran, Roseville Park at Dubbo, Towalba at Peak Hill, the famous Haddon Rig stud and probably another thirty or so studs in the general region.

I would have a lot of catching up to do if Mrs Gordon was prepared to sell it to me. Over the many years I'd been catching crooks and advising companies about security measures, the owners of these studs had been improving their sheep – putting more meat on them to make the merino more of a dual purpose sheep. Stuart hadn't put this same effort into our sheep because he was keener on cattle. But here I'd be in the loop, so to speak, and could measure our sheep against the best the other studs could produce. Dubbo was also a great place for showing off cattle because they held big cattle shows there.

'If you sell me Glengarry you won't have to worry about a clearing sale of your goods. I'll get a valuer to come and put a price on everything and buy the property on a walk-in walk-out basis. Anything you want, you take,' I said.

'I'd definitely be taking Jock and Jimbo,' she said.

Jock was Harry's last dog, a black and tan Kelpie, while Jimbo was the monstrous and most certainly neutered black and white cat who followed Mrs Gordon like a shadow.

She invited me into her lounge room and we sat there for a while in silence. I held my breath because I sensed she was on the verge of making a decision. Presently she nodded. 'I'd be very happy for you to buy Glengarry and I think Harry would be too.'

'Thank you so much,' I said. 'I'll make sure I justify your faith in me. Would you mind me delaying closing on the sale for a couple of days, Mrs Gordon? There's a certain woman in my life who's waiting very anxiously to hear from me. I wouldn't like to make as big a decision as this without her being happy about it.'

'Very wise too. Of course you must let your friend come and see Glengarry,' she said.

'I'll try and get her to drive up tomorrow unless she'd prefer to fly to Dubbo and meet me there,' I said.

I went outside and dialled Gaye on her mobile. 'I think I've found the place for us, Gaye. It's called Glengarry and it's in the Gilgandra area. It's around 4000 acres and the owner, a Mrs Gordon, is prepared to sell it to me. Can you get up tomorrow? If you don't want to drive you could get the plane to Dubbo and I'll meet you at the airport.'

'That's wonderful news. It's probably easier if I fly up. I'll ring now and see if I can get a seat,' she said.

Gaye was able to get a flight and arrived in Dubbo the next day. After lunch we drove out to Glengarry and I introduced Gaye to Mrs Gordon, and they chatted away. After a cup of tea, we set off on another tour of the property with Mrs Gordon guiding us.

'When we arrived back at the house Mrs Gordon went back into the homestead and I walked Gaye around the buildings, finishing up near the old stables. 'If we take it,' I said, 'I'll get a bush carpenter to build you a new set of stables. And it's fairly hot here in summer so I think we could run to an in-ground pool. What do you think?' I asked.

'Oh, yes. The house is great and I'm in love with the pantry. Did you ever see so many preserves? The orchard is a plus and the garden wouldn't be hard to keep in order. I think you should buy it, Lachie. It's big enough, isn't it?' Gaye asked.

'Quite,' I agreed. So we went to Mrs Gordon and told her that we would like to buy Glengarry at market value on a walk-in, walk-out arrangement and that she could take whatever she wanted.

I could see that our decision to Mrs Gordon was a real relief because she would be absolved from any worry about the sale. To sell or not to sell had been her constant worry. She couldn't run the place and if she sold now before she was too decrepit she and her sister might be able to manage the trip they wanted to take to her husband's ancestral country in Scotland. She and Harry had always wanted to go there do but never had the time.

Mrs Gordon was aware that I was staying at the Alpha motel in Gilgandra but it didn't stop her from inviting Gaye to stay the night with her. I think she wanted a good old chinwag with her. Gaye looked at me and I nodded. How could I be disappointed when Mrs Gordon had just sold me her property?

Before I left Glengarry I walked around the lucerne paddock and saw in my mind's eye where I would build the cattle shed. I also thought I'd add to the woolshed so that show sheep could be transferred quite easily for shearing. But that was all in the future and there was a lot to do before I could think about showing sheep.

EPILOGUE

Gaye stood with me as the last semitrailer unloaded the final run of my Kamilaroi ewes. I'd had to cull them heavily because there were a great deal more than I'd be able to run on Glengarry. A hundred and fifty Hereford cows had arrived the previous day and were grazing contentedly in the river paddocks. We'd had to renovate and enlarge the sheep yards to cater for the sheep but it was a job well done.

'Well, there you are, Mrs Sinclair,' I said as we watched the last ewes string out across the paddock. 'Glengarry is stocked now. When you get your horses you'll be able to ride out and keep an eye on the sheep.'

Gaye looked across to where some men were working on new stables and yards so we could bring some horses onto Glengarry again.

'It's worked out well in the finish,' said Gaye, smiling as she took my hand.

Flora and Laurie had bought my third of Kamilaroi and I'd given them a special deal on the cattle and sheep left over after I'd taken my share. They'd used Flora's third of Kamilaroi to finance the purchase of my block. They were going to pay Stuart to look after both blocks. It now looked as if Stuart might be able to raise the money to give Nicole her half of what he owned. So there was a very good chance that Kamilaroi might remain intact.

'This will be more fun than chasing baddies,' I said.

'Heaps more,' she agreed. 'Especially when I beat you shearing a sheep.'

'Only by a blow,' I said.

The future looked decidedly promising.

AUTHOR'S NOTE

The police personnel in this story attributed to Coonabarabran Police Station never existed nor is the station of this story meant to be a facsimile of the Coonabarabran establishment. It is a station of the Mudgee police sub-district. During 1972 I was news editor and rural reporter for the 2BS-2MG radio stations. One of my duties entailed visiting the Mudgee Police Station at least once, and sometimes twice, every day. I covered a bank hold-up, a jail break, innumerable road fatalities, domestic problems, stock theft, minor and major burglaries and many other misdemeanours. I am happy to say, albeit belatedly, that I was always treated with great courtesy and given all possible assistance. For this I must acknowledge Superintendent Rees and sergeants Elliott, McLeod and Milton. I had a very happy time at Mudgee and this was due in no small measure to the help I received from every officer of the Mudgee station.

Back to the Pilliga is, to some extent anyway, a long-delayed thankyou for the above assistance while also acknowledging the role of police in the maintenance of law and order in great areas of country. If I have taken some liberties in the telling of this story, I hope it will be accepted that it was done with the very best of intentions.

Tony Parsons OAM
East Greenmount, Queensland